"If a man isn't smart enough to love you for yourself, who needs him?"

It sounded so right coming from Jace. "So we're the walking wounded?" Melonie asked.

"My scars are healed, but I am most assuredly gun-shy," he said firmly. "Besides, we've been busy enough the past couple of years that it didn't much matter." He stood and rolled his shoulders, and she tried to pretend he didn't look absolutely amazing when he did it. "Now with kids to raise, my focus needs to be on them."

"Agreed." She stood, too.

He stayed right there, looking at her.

She looked right back.

"So why is my focus longing to shift, Melonie?" Jace whispered the words, gazing at her. Into her eyes.

Was his heart slow-tripping like hers? Were his palms growing damp?

Stop this. You know better. You know your plans. You're leaving as soon as you've secured your inheritance. His life is here. Yours isn't. And there are two baby girls to consider...

Multipublished bestselling author **Ruth Logan Herne** loves God, her country, her family, dogs, chocolate and coffee! Married to a very patient man, she lives in an old farmhouse in upstate New York and thinks possums should leave the cat food alone and snakes should always live outside. There are no exceptions to either rule! Visit Ruth at ruthloganherne.com.

Books by Ruth Logan Herne

Love Inspired

Shepherd's Crossing

Her Cowboy Reunion
A Cowboy in Shepherd's Crossing

Grace Haven

An Unexpected Groom
Her Unexpected Family
Their Surprise Daddy
The Lawman's Yuletide Baby
Her Secret Daughter

Kirkwood Lake

The Lawman's Second Chance
Falling for the Lawman
The Lawman's Holiday Wish
Loving the Lawman
Her Holiday Family

Visit the Author Profile page at Harlequin.com for more titles.

A Cowboy in Shepherd's Crossing

Ruth Logan Herne

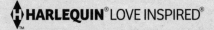

HARLEQUIN® LOVE INSPIRED®

Recycling programs
for this product may
not exist in your area.

LOVE INSPIRED BOOKS

ISBN-13: 978-1-335-53893-2

A Cowboy in Shepherd's Crossing

www.Harlequin.com

Printed in U.S.A.

Judge not, and ye shall not be judged:
condemn not, and ye shall not be condemned:
forgive, and ye shall be forgiven.
—*Luke* 6:37

This book is dedicated to Christina,
a wonderful young woman who won my heart
from the very beginning… Thank you
for becoming a true "overcomer." Your story
is the kind of thing that inspires others
to do their best. To try harder. To never give up.
I love you, kid.

Chapter One

The last thing Jace Middleton wanted was to leave the place he loved so well. The place he knew, the town he'd called home for nearly thirty years and the land that beckoned him like a cow calls a calf. But the town had fallen on hard times, and the choices he wanted no longer existed in Shepherd's Crossing.

He ran one hand across the nape of his neck as he studied the family farmhouse that had been passed down for three generations. Three generations that ended with him.

He shoved emotions aside and studied the old house from a builder's perspective. The faded gray house lacked...everything.

Not the essentials. The modest one-and-a-half-story home was solidly built, and the mid-twentieth-century addition nearly doubled the first-floor living space, but there was nothing about this house that tempted folks to make an offer anywhere near his asking price. The way Jace saw things playing out, he would be left with two choices.

Walk away, begin life anew in Sun Valley and let the Realtor handle it. Or fix the place up, except…

He sighed.

He couldn't do it. He was good at tearing apart other folks' things and putting them back together. The thought made him flex his arms. There was nothing Jace liked better than reconfiguring something old into something new, but every time he went to change something in his parents' home, he ground to a stop. These were family walls. Family memories. They belonged to him and his younger sister, Justine.

These walls held all he had left of his parents, Jason and Ivy Middleton. He'd lost one to cancer and the other one to heartbreak, and he couldn't bring himself to demolish one stinking part of this house, even to increase the resale value. It felt wrong. Plain wrong. But he was slated to begin a new job in Sun Valley by Labor Day, which meant he had a couple of months to get things in order, sell the unsellable house, pay off his sister's college loans and start fresh. With dwindling jobs, cash and population, there was little left in Shepherd's Crossing, and things had grown worse over time.

He needed a fresh start.

He pretended he didn't downright hate that thought as a stylish SUV pulled into the nearby intersection. The car started to turn left, then paused.

It pulled back, onto the main road. Then the driver cranked the wheel in the opposite direction.

She paused again, looking left, then right, then frowned down at something... A map? A GPS?

Jace had no idea but every now and again a stormy day messed up satellite signals so he started her way about the same time she banked a sharp left turn and spotted him. She pulled up in front of the house, climbed out and came his way, leaving her car running in the middle of the road. Not pulled off to the edge like normal folks do, but smack-dab in the middle of the road, hogging the northbound lane. Who did things like that?

Tall, beautiful, well-dressed women who think they own the world, he decided as she crossed the driveway looking way too fine for their humble little town. He'd done a stint with a worldly woman a few years back, and one high-heeled heart-stomping had been more than enough.

"Your car." He pointed behind her as she

approached. "You might want to move it off the road."

"I won't be long." Strong. Self-assured. And cucumber-cool. So already annoying. "You're selling this place?"

Was she a would-be buyer? If that was the case, she could leave her car wherever she wanted and he'd be crazy polite. "Yes."

"What's the asking price?"

He told her and she lifted an eyebrow. "How long has it been on the market?"

Longer than it should have taken, but he wasn't about to admit that to her. "A few weeks."

She waited, watching him, as if she knew he was downscaling the time frame.

"Six weeks, actually."

Her look went from him to the house and back as two cars came down the road. She paid no attention to the cars, or the fact that they needed to get around her car to make it into the intersection. She moved forward, toward the house, then paused. "This is your place?"

"Yes."

"Do you want advice?"

"Not if it requires me changing anything." It was a stupid answer, and he knew it, but he couldn't bring himself to pretend.

"I see." She gave him a smile that was half-polite and half something that wasn't one bit polite. "Well, best of luck to you."

She crossed back to her car, waited at the road while another car buzzed by, then took her place behind the wheel. He thought she was going to put it in gear and go, but she paused. Looked back at him. "I'm going to Pine Ridge Ranch. Do you know where that is?"

He shoved his cowboy hat back on his head and choked down a sigh.

He knew all right. He'd spent the last dozen years working there with his friend Heath Caufield. This must be the middle Fitzgerald sister, come to stake a claim on the ranch. He knew that because her sister Lizzie told him she'd be along soon.

This sister was different, though. Smoky gray eyes, dark curly hair and skin the color of biscuit-toned porcelain, a current popular choice in kitchens and baths. Lizzie failed to mention that her sister thought herself a cut above, so his work time on the ranch just got a little more tedious than it needed to be. "I'm heading there right now. I'll take lead. You follow."

"Or just tell me how to get there," she replied in a voice that suggested she wasn't about to follow anyone anywhere.

So be it. He did a slow count to five before he let her have it her way. "Two miles up the road, give or take, a left turn into a winding drive that heads deeper into the valley. There's a mailbox that marks the spot."

"Great. Thanks." She put the car into gear and drove off.

He got into his worn pickup truck, turned it around and followed her, and when he parked the truck at the ranch about five minutes later, her stylish SUV was nowhere to be seen.

"Jace, you want to run the baler now that the dew's burned off? That first cutting of hay looks mighty nice this year." Heath Caufield came his way and Jace nodded as he shut the truck door.

"Glad to. Hey, buddy. What's up?" Jace high-fived Heath's son when the five-year-old raced over to him—the child seemed unhampered by the neon-green cast on his right forearm.

"We're having another baby horse, and a wedding!" shrieked Zeke. He barreled into Jace's arms and gave him a big hug. "And you're goin' to be with Daddy when he gets married and then my Lizzie gets to be my mom like every…single…day." He paused between words to magnify their importance, and Jace understood real well how nice it was to have a mom. And how much you missed them once they were gone.

"Zeke." Heath made a face at the boy. "I'm supposed to *ask* Jace to stand up with me at the wedding. Not boss him around."

Zeke put his little hands over his face and giggled. "Oops. Sorry! Hey, somebody's coming, Dad!" He pointed up the hill as the white SUV made its way into the valley. Dust rose from the graveled drive, blanketing the car, and when it finally made its way into the barnyard, the sleek white paint wore a film of fine Idaho dirt.

The door opened. The woman got out, and waited for the dust to clear. When it did, she spotted Jace right off. "You beat me here."

He may have smirked slightly. "The turnoff could be better marked, I suppose."

Her eyes narrowed, but then she spotted Heath.

She smiled then, and Jace was pretty sure it was about the prettiest smile he'd ever seen. Fitzgerald eyes, about the only thing she had in common with her uncle Sean and her sister Lizzie.

"Melonie?" Heath started forward. "Gosh, it's great to see you. Lizzie will be over the moon that you're here. And this big guy—" Heath set his hand on the five-year-old's head "—is my son, Zeke."

"We've met over the computer." Lizzie's sister bent to the boy's level and offered him a sweet smile. "But you're even more handsome in real life, Zeke Caufield."

Zeke grinned, clearly charmed in less time than a foolish man takes to ride a rodeo bull.

Heath clapped the boy on the back and laughed. "Lizzie's at the horse stables, but she'll be right along. How are you?" he asked as the woman stepped forward and gave him a hug.

"Ask me in twelve months when I can take my career off hold," she told him. She lifted her eyebrows toward the beautiful horse stables just west of the graveled parking area. "If I live that long. You know me and horses—we learned the hard way to stay clear of one another and that's not about to change. Sakes alive, Heath." She gazed around and her eyes softened with appreciation. Her voice drawled now, a nod to the woman's Southern roots. Funny there was no trace of that drawl when she'd stopped at Jace's place. "This has got to be the back door to nowhere, isn't it? And yet... It's real pretty in its own Western way."

Back door to nowhere?

Jace hung back, purposely.

He knew her kind, all right. The sort that kept themselves separate, disparaging the dawn-to-dusk hard work on a spread like this. The kind of woman that found down-home ranching beneath them. His family had helped settle this town. They'd built homes, dug wells and arranged for schooling and libraries, and they'd done it all expecting nothing in return except a chance to grow a town worth living in, so he not only respected the work that went into this town. He admired it.

"Jace." Heath motioned him over and it would be rude to stand still. Rude…but tempting, none-theless. He rebuffed the temptation and crossed between the vehicles. "Jace, this is Lizzie's sister, Melonie. Mel, this is my friend and right-hand man, Jace Middleton."

"Mr. Middleton." She drawled his name out with all the pomp of a modern day Scarlett O'Hara and if that didn't spell trouble with a capital *T*, then nothing did. "It is a pleasure to make your official acquaintance."

"Mine, too, ma'am." He extended his hand. She met his gaze, straight on, then took his hand. The strength of her grip surprised him but he refused to show it. "Glad you found your way. Eventually."

"As am I." He was pretty sure the Southern drawl was all for his benefit because it disap-peared when Lizzie came running across the grass from the stables.

"Melonie!"

"Lizzie!" They hugged and laughed and at that moment he couldn't resent her because he knew what it was like to have family love.

You knew it, you mean.

He choked down a sigh. He started for the baler, wishing things were different. He wished the town's economy hadn't started to nose-dive two decades back when no one bothered looking. Wished he wasn't the last Middleton in a town built by Middletons.

But he was, and there were no two ways about it. Jace was going to do the one thing he hated to do. He was going to leave Shepherd's Crossing and all his family had built over the years. Built…and lost.

He yanked his cowboy hat onto his head and fired up the baler. He'd longed for a chance to set things right, to make a name for himself in his hometown, but that wasn't about to happen now.

So be it.

He'd do whatever it took to help his kid sister, Justine, get the start she deserved, and to make his way in the world. Even if it meant changing up the old house. He pushed the thoughts aside as he maneuvered the big machine out of the equipment barn to gas it up.

Lizzie's sister looked up. Not at him, but beyond him. Something marked her gaze. Something shadowed and maybe even sad as her eyes swept over the beautiful ranch with a long, slow look. A look that indicated she was in the wrong place at the wrong time. She righted her features before she turned back toward Lizzie, but then she saw him looking her way.

Her gaze narrowed. Her mouth did, too. But

the face she showed Lizzie two seconds later was warm and genuine.

Only it wasn't, and right now Jace Middleton was pretty sure only he and Melonie Fitzgerald knew that.

Sparse population, drastically cold winters and a herd of horses probably waiting to trample her senseless.

What on earth was Melonie Fitzgerald doing in western Idaho, when she'd been on the verge of contracting her own home-design TV show?

She knew the answer. Her father. He was a major publishing owner/executive who'd brought down his company, his home and his three daughters when he diverted millions in cold, hard cash into overseas accounts…then followed it there.

She didn't do ranches. She steered clear of horses for good reason. And when her long-term boyfriend realized she was not only broke, but also in a mountain of debt, he'd dumped her like a hot potato fresh out of the coals.

Yet here she was, fulfilling the terms of a bequest on her late uncle's ranch when she should have been on camera, filming the pilot episode of *Shoestring Southern Charm*.

Girl, you make the best of every situation. If it gets dark, you light a candle. If it gets cold,

start a fire, or warm a room with your smile. A
smile goes a lot further than a frown.

Corrie's words. Succinct and true, always de-
pendable. She turned to ask Lizzie about their
nanny/surrogate mother, but caught the cowboy's
gaze instead.

He was hot. Not big-city hot, either. Country
hot, with his long-sleeved blue thermal shirt,
dark blue jeans and a to-die-for real cowboy hat.
The black hat showed off his bronze skin and
made him look even more rugged, if such a thing
was possible.

He'd duped her over the directions.

After you treated him like a back-road hick.

She winced because she'd iced him and she
wasn't usually like that. But four years of running part of the magazine's corporate office had
affected her. She faced her sister. "Where's Corrie?"

"Up the drive visiting Rosie and the baby."

Was Melonie supposed to have a clue what
she meant? Because she didn't.

Lizzie took her arm as the good-looking cowboy busied himself with a fairly monstrous piece
of machinery. "You'll get to know folks quick
enough. There are a lot of nice people here, Mel."

Mel locked eyes with her. "There are nice people everywhere. Doesn't mean I intend to live
there. You know me. This isn't exactly my thing."

"And on that note." Heath slipped an arm around Lizzie, kissed her, then bumped his forehead to hers. "I'll be back tomorrow. Love you."

Lizzie gave him a smile that said more than words. "Love you, too. See you tomorrow."

"Yeah, see you, Dad!" The brown-skinned little boy jumped into his father's arms and gave Heath a big hug. "Maybe we'll make some cookies for you. Okay?"

"Okay." Heath shared a grin with the boy, then took off in a muscled-out pickup truck.

"They're taking the winter lambs to market." Melonie scowled. "I know what that means."

"Says the steak lover in the family."

Melonie started to acknowledge that, but spotted Corrie coming their way. She dropped her purse and raced off to meet the woman who'd stood by the three sisters for as long as she could remember.

"Have mercy, I've missed you, girl!" Corrie pulled back, looked Mel over, then offered her a sweet, wide smile. "Look at you, all Louisville fancy in the heart of western Idaho."

"Please do not tell me this is overdressed," said Mel. She glanced at Lizzie's blue jeans, barn boots and T-shirt and sighed. "Never mind."

"I've got stuff you can use, Mel. But yeah, even casual silk has no place here." Lizzie exchanged a grin with Corrie. "And cotton's a must."

"Meaning I might as well leave my luggage in the car, right?"

Corrie laughed. "Let's get your things inside and we'll catch up. Did Cottonwood Productions offer you a contract? And are they willing to wait?"

"Yes and no." Melonie pushed a lock of hair out of her eyes as she trundled a bag up the steps. "When they realized I had to be here, they quietly shredded the whole thing."

"Oh, Mel." Lizzie stopped on the top step. "That could have been a huge step forward for you. Wasn't it worth foregoing Uncle Sean's bequest to give it a shot?"

Melonie shook her head as she climbed the stairs. "Breaking into cable is high risk. Most pilots go nowhere. Only a few make it, but with nothing to live on, the choice became a no-brainer. Ezra is shopping it around, but I've got bills to pay." Ezra had been a photographer for the magazine. Now he was working freelance photography and videography.

"I hear you," said Lizzie. "Come on in, let's get you settled. And I don't know about the two of you, but I'm hungry. Let's make some sandwiches and eat them on the porch with the cute kid. We can play with the puppies."

Cute kid. Puppies. Sandwiches?

Was this her low-carb, former publishing-executive sister talking? The one whose job disappeared along with their swindling father? She reached out a hand to Lizzie's forehead. "No fever, but possible delirium. Who are you and what have you done with my sister?"

Lizzie laughed as Zeke popped in, grabbed a cookie, then headed right back out again. "I'm a rancher, Mel. Welcome to the Pine Ridge Ranch. It is—" she slipped an arm around Melonie's shoulders and gave her a half hug as they moved to the stairs "—real nice to have you on board. I'm hoping you'll be surprised by the reception you get when you meet the locals. I gave all kinds of people the last two copies of your magazine and they loved them. Who knows?" She lifted the suitcase to carry it up the stairs. "You might land some jobs here."

Melonie had gotten an eyeful of what Shepherd's Crossing had to offer when she shot past the farm drive on her first pass through. The small town just north of Pine Ridge featured worn-out buildings, paint-peeling facades and a pervading air of desperation. Not exactly a recipe for success.

She could make a difference. She knew that instantly, but she had no stake, no cash and no reserves to draw on. For a design person like her, Shepherd's Crossing would be a fresh canvas.

She'd love to engage her hands in a project like that, to help renovate a run-down community.

But she'd found out the hard way that nothing came from nothing, and without money... Well, there were no options without money.

"Ladies."

That voice. Jace's voice, ringing deep and strong and true. She came face-to-face with him as he crossed the broad front porch. She moved to the screen door and pointed. "They're taking my things upstairs. Can I help?"

"Let Lizzie know we'll be running hay all day. Have her text if she needs me between loads."

"I will. And hey—I was short with you when I stopped by your place. I'm sorry."

"No harm done."

"There was," she insisted, opening the screen door. For some reason she wanted him to understand. "Generally I'm a nice person. Except around horses and dirt and manure."

He didn't smile at the joke. He looked almost sorry for her, then put up his hands. "Apology accepted. Those of us who work around all three on a daily basis will be sure to steer clear."

That wasn't what she meant and only a thin-skinned, stubborn, boneheaded man would take it that way. A man with the greatest set of shoulders she'd ever seen.

He walked away, climbed onto the big machine and started it up. Then he rumbled it past the barns, down a long lane stretching to far-away fields. And he didn't look back.

Chapter Two

Jace parked the baler midafternoon and headed toward the ranch house for lunch. Bob "Cookie" Cook managed the ranch kitchen. He was gone for the day, but he'd texted that he'd left a platter of meat, cheese and sandwich fixings in the kitchen, along with a bowl of potato salad. After five hours of baling the important first cutting of hay, he and the others would get the hay under cover before the predicted overnight rain. Wet hay fostered mold growth, so they'd be running the hay wagons back and forth from the field to the hay barns and lofts until dark…and maybe after. It wouldn't be the first time he'd hauled hay in the dark.

He climbed the steps and met two of the other hands in the kitchen. Harve Jr. was building a sandwich and Wick was already plowing into a monster-sized plate of potato salad. He saw the women on the front porch, laughing together, but the cool reprieve of the kitchen offered more invitation. He'd taken his first bite when the crunch of tires on gravel drew the men's attention. From his seat, he spotted Gilda Hardaway, the grumpy eccentric who lived in a sprawling, decaying house on an empty ranch near the Payette National Forest. She approached the porch, looking testier than ever.

But then the front door opened. Lizzie came in. She spotted him and motioned him forward.

Wick and Harve Jr. exchanged grins, glad they weren't summoned.

He stood, swiped his mouth with a piece of paper towel and walked to the porch. "Ladies." He tipped his head in their direction. "What can I do for you?"

"Not them. Me, young man."

He was afraid of that. He faced Gilda. "Well, how can I be of help, Mrs. Hardaway?"

She looked him up and down as if he was a science exhibit. Then she sighed. "Can I come inside or do I have to air dirty laundry out here where any Tom, Dick or Harry might overhear?"

"Of course," Lizzie answered. She opened the white, wooden screen door and let the old woman precede her. Then she sent Jace a questioning look.

He shrugged, because he didn't know any more than she did.

"We should sit down," said the old woman.

Jace didn't want to sit. He wanted to eat his lunch and get back to work. He was on a tight schedule. One band of sheep was still in the hills, and Heath and two other hands were loading lambs for market on the far side of the mountain. Already he heard noise in the kitchen, meaning the other men had wolfed down their food and were ready to haul. One look at Gilda Hardaway nixed his choices. He sat.

The old woman lifted a magazine from the coffee table. She held it up to Lizzie. "That your sister out there on the porch? This one?" She waggled the magazine.

Lizzie nodded.

"We'll need her in here."

Jace watched Lizzie fight whatever she wanted to say, because Lizzie wasn't the kind of woman anyone bossed around. But she kept her lips pressed tight, then called Melonie and Corrie in. If the old woman didn't want Corrie on hand, she at least had the grace not to show it.

Once the other two women had taken seats, Mrs. Hardaway turned back toward him. "Your name is not Jace Middleton."

Well, that explained the unexplainable visit.

She'd gone batty. Clearly batty because he knew who he was.

"Your father was Lionel Tate."

Lionel Tate was his father's cousin. He'd left town a long time ago and died somewhere. Jace didn't remember where because he'd never known the man. "My father was Jason Middleton."

The old woman's frown deepened. "Jason and Ivy took you in as a baby. You were just over a year old, and when they offered to take you in, it was agreed upon because it fit."

Hairs began to rise along the nape of Jace's neck. What was she talking about?

"Your mother was angry when Lionel left. Very angry. She handed you over and went off on her own. As far as I know, no one heard from her until she showed back up nine years later with a baby girl."

"Mrs. Hardaway, I believe you're confused." He kept his voice calm as he offered an explanation. "Justine is six years younger than me. She's just finished her master's in biochemistry and she's doing a paid internship in Seattle."

"Your *other* sister," she told him. "Your biological half sister. She is younger than you by nearly eleven years."

The firmness in her voice—the staunch look

in her eye, as if she was the one who was right—unnerved him. "Mrs. Hardaway…"

Lizzie put a hand on his arm. Her sister darted a look from him to the old woman and back, as if embarrassed for him. Or her. Or just plain embarrassed to be there.

"She gave that baby up for adoption, too, because she came here and no one stepped in to take care of that baby girl, and there's plenty of shame to go around about that. When your folks offered to take her in, too, seeing as she was your sister, they were told 'no' because of tough family finances."

She wasn't making sense, and yet… He remembered hushed whispers around that time. He'd been plenty old enough to realize something was going on, but never knew what. Snips of private conversation came back to him, conversations that meant nothing then…and everything at this moment. "That makes no sense, because we weren't poor. My mother was a schoolteacher and Dad was a contractor. He worked all the time. We were always financially solid."

She locked her eyes with his, then said something that tipped everything into sharper focus. "Your sister is white."

And there it was. A divide he'd never personally felt in Shepherd's Crossing because the Middletons had been some of the earliest pioneers in the area. But now—

A mix of raw emotions began churning inside him. "How can that be, Mrs. Hardaway?"

She held his gaze, held it hard, as if this whole thing hurt her more than it pained him. Then she spoke, and he understood the wounded expression. "Because I am your grandmother, Jace. And my daughter Barbara was…" Her mouth trembled slightly. And her eyes looked sad. "Your mother."

None of this could be true.

It couldn't.

He'd seen his birth certificate. He had it, back at the house. "You're wrong, I'm afraid. I have proof of who I am at my home. My family home, Mrs. Hardaway." He stood, ready to end this nonsense and get to work.

"Your birth certificate," she said.

He nodded. "It lists everything. Mother. Father. Date and time of birth. Place of birth. We're haying today, but if you give me a day or two, I'll bring it by so you can see it for yourself." Whatever had happened back then, he had government-certified proof of who he was. Clearly the old woman was mistaken.

"It is the practice in many states to alter the birth certificates of adopted children, Jace. Adoptions back then were meant to be private affairs for a reason. I have the original certificate here." She reached into an old purse and withdrew a folded, faded sheet of paper. Then she handed it over.

He didn't want to look at it.

What if it was true?

He unfolded the paper and read the information there. And his heart chugged to a slow, draining stop in his chest.

"Jace." Lizzie had stood, too. She gripped his arm gently.

He read his birth date.

The time of birth, the place—all exactly the same as his certificate at home. But the names were different. He swallowed hard, wanting to shove the paper back at her and walk out the door. Wanting—

"I know this is hard, but there's a reason I'm here today." The old woman hunched forward. "I have things to fix."

Not on his dime.

He set down the paper. He didn't crumple it and throw it back at her, which is what he wanted to do. No. He set it down and started for the door.

"Jace." The old woman stood and began to hobble after him. She looked frantic, but he didn't care. He didn't care one bit, he—

"I'm not looking for forgiveness." She rasped

the words and his heart lurched. "I'm looking for help. For labor."

None of this was making sense, but he turned back. "Listen, Mrs. Hardaway…"

"Gilda. Please." She held out a picture of the old, rambling house on Hardaway Ranch. The place must have been a beauty in its time, but that was a generation or two back. Now it was a neglected wreck with a grumpy recluse living inside. "I had to tell you the truth, Jace, because I need you. Your sister's gone off, leaving her two babies. If we don't step in and do something to claim those little girls, they'll end up in foster care. And I can't let another wrong go unchecked."

Now she had his attention. "What do you mean about my sister? About babies?"

"Valencia." Corrie breathed the word softly. She folded her hands tight in her lap, as if praying.

"You know her?" asked Mrs. Hardaway.

"I have met her twice, but it's the children I know best. Two beautiful children, twin girls. Ava and Annie. Rosie watches them here on the ranch. But I believe that Valencia has a mother working at the Carrington Ranch. Correct?"

"She did, but she's left there and gone to Florida. Lora Garcia is her adoptive mother and she wants nothing to do with Valencia or those children," Gilda told them. "She has made that clear. But I cannot turn my back on another child. I've done that three times." She stood and locked eyes with Jace. "I must make amends, but my house is unlivable for children."

"You're thinking of taking these children?" This reclusive woman could barely care for herself. "Impossible. If what you say is true—"

"It is," she interrupted firmly, then waited.

He prayed.

In his head, quiet as can be, he prayed because right now he had no idea what to do. Except he knew he couldn't turn over two small children to an elderly woman with health issues and a laundry list of regrets regarding children already. He'd seen the two little girls at Rosie's house a time or two. He hadn't thought much of it. Now he'd be able to think of nothing else. "I will take charge of the children." He thought he glimpsed a gleam of approval in her eye, but if he did, it was short-lived. "Unless you have objections to their dark uncle taking charge."

She flinched, but then shook her head. "No objections at all. I don't have energy for little children, I'm not what they need, but I've got money."

He didn't need her money. "I—"

She raised a hand "To hire you. And her." She poked a finger toward Lizzie's very surprised sister and Melonie's eyes opened wide. "To make a difference. I want my house to be beautiful again. To be a place I can be proud to leave for these children. It's time I took charge, Jace. And I've seen your work." She tapped the magazine as she drew Melonie into the conversation. "It's remarkable and inviting. I want you to do the designing." She turned to face Jace again. "I want you to make her designs come true. If you can both look at the project once the hay is in the barn, you can come up with an estimate and I'll give you start-up costs. Then we'll have begun to fix two things. My great-grandchildren will have a place to live. And maybe the ranch won't look sad and lonely anymore."

Renovate her home. Her ranch. Take on the custody of twin toddlers he didn't know.

Six hours ago he'd lamented his lack of family in Shepherd's Crossing.

What a joke. Because now he seemed to have more family than he knew what to do with…

He caught Melonie's eyes across the room. She had the grace to stay quiet, but what choice did he have?

He turned toward Lizzie and Corrie. "I've got to help get the hay in. Rain's expected and my house isn't ready for two little kids. Can I impose—"

Melonie stood up. "It's no imposition. You

can have my room here. I'll bunk in the stable with Lizzie." She faced her sister. "There's room, isn't there?"

"Always, Mel. It will be like old times," Lizzie said quietly. "The horses won't bother you?"

"Not as long as they stay downstairs."

They'd thrown him a lifeline. A lifeline he'd gladly take hold of. "I'd be grateful," Jace told them. "Just until I can get things right at the house. And—" he turned toward Melonie and had to eat his words from that morning "—the advice you offered this morning?"

"About your house?"

The sudden addition of two toddlers negated his reluctance to change things up. "I'm ready to take it."

He went through the door and didn't look back. The women would sort things out with Gilda, and they'd be more diplomatic than he could be right now.

He crossed to the hay stacker, climbed in and turned it on. He spotted Wick and young Harve making bales in the far field. He aimed the stacker that way while his mind churned on what he'd just heard.

He hated that it made sense. He hated that the two wonderful, faith-filled people he loved weren't really his parents and had never trusted him enough to tell him. Why would they keep this a secret? It wasn't like there was shame in adoption.

He'd been hoping for local jobs to crop up again. He'd said that often enough, and here was a mammoth one being laid at his feet, a job that hinged on something he'd never much thought of until just now. The color of his skin and the accidents of birth.

His grandmother hadn't wanted him thirty years ago. She'd made sure he was tucked in with a lovely black family because it fit.

And now it didn't.

His phone buzzed. He pulled it out. Glanced down. I scheduled a meeting with Gilda Hardaway for 3:00 p.m. tomorrow. Okay?

It was from Melonie Fitzgerald, telling him what to do and how to do it. Could this possibly get any worse?

He sighed, texted back Yes and shoved the phone away because he was pretty sure it could get worse.

And there wasn't a thing he could do about it.

Chapter Three

Two borrowed portable cribs.

A mountain-sized stack of disposable diapers.

Creams, lotions, shampoos and bottles. Lots of bottles. Two babies had just moved into the ranch house.

Melonie Fitzgerald had never changed a diaper in her life. Nor had she cared to.

By hour three she'd changed two under Corrie's watchful eye. "Done." She set the wriggling girl onto the floor and stood up to wash her hands.

The baby burst into tears. Big, loud tears.

Then the second one noted her sister's agony and followed suit. The babies looked around the room at all the strange faces and kept right on crying.

"Here, sweetie." Lizzie picked up one. Corrie lifted the other. And still they cried.

"Mel, Rosie brought bottles ready to warm. Can you do that for us?"

"Sure." She slipped into the kitchen, took out the bottles and stared at them. Then she picked up her smartphone and asked it how to warm a baby's bottle while the twins howled in the front room.

No answer and they had two screaming babies and a perfectly good microwave. She searched for directions.

Oops. Microwave warming was not recommended…but desperate times called for desperate measures. She followed the non-recommended directions, made sure the formula wasn't too hot, shook it and tested it again, then recapped the bottles.

"Mel?" Lizzie's voice sounded desperate.

"Coming." She brought the bottles into the great room and handed one to Lizzie and the other to Corrie, but Corrie surprised her. "You take charge of this one."

"Me?"

Corrie nodded as she tucked the baby into Melonie's arms. "I promised Zeke I'd take him to play with the puppies. We don't want him to feel left out."

"Corrie, thank you." Lizzie looked up from the straight-backed chair and Melonie was glad she didn't look any more skilled than Melonie felt at that moment. "We'll get the hang of this. Won't we, Mel?"

Don't say what you're thinking. Just smile and nod.

She did and Lizzie grinned, because Lizzie always knew what Mel was thinking. She sat down primly and posed the nipple near the baby's mouth.

The baby… Ava, maybe? Or Annie? She wasn't sure so she peeked at the baby's arm.

Ava. She knew because she'd surreptitiously put a tiny dot on her right forearm.

The baby grabbed hold of that bottle, yanked it into her mouth and proceeded to drink as if starvation was on the horizon. From the looks of the wee one's chunky thighs, Melonie was pretty sure her desperation was vastly overdone.

"Are they supposed to be this big?" she whispered to Lizzie. "They're like monster-sized."

Lizzie burst out laughing. "I was thinking the same thing. But Rosie said they're ten months old, so that's almost a year. And Rosie has been taking wonderful care of them. And she said she's happy to continue being their nanny while we all work."

Work.

Melonie drew up a mental image of the picture Gilda Hardaway had flashed her way. The two-and-a-half-story home was a skeleton of its former self, but with help...

"This is them?"

Jace's voice drew her gaze. He was framed in the screen door, looking every bit as good as he had that morning, which meant she needed to work harder to ignore it. He opened the door and walked in. Once inside, he glanced from one baby to the next and she wasn't sure if he was going to run screaming or cry.

He did neither.

He set that big, black cowboy hat on a small table, crouched down in front of her and Baby Number One and smiled.

Oh, that smile.

Melonie's heart did a skip-jump that would have done an Irish dancer proud. She quashed it instantly. She was here to do her part, whatever that might be, and then leave. Her dream wasn't here in the craggy hills of western Idaho. It resided south, in the warm, rolling streets of Kentucky and Tennessee, where she yearned to show folks how to create a pocketbook-friendly version of Southern charm.

He started to reach out for the baby, but then his phone rang. He glanced at the display and made a face. "Justine." He turned to face Lizzie. "How do I explain all this to my kid sister?"

"The same way it got explained to us," she

said softly. "But first." She stood and crossed the room, then handed him the baby. "Let Justine go to voice mail for a few minutes. Meet your niece. This is Ava."

Melonie frowned. "That's Annie. This is Ava."

Lizzie frowned, too. "No, I'm sure that—"

Melonie shifted the sleeve of the baby's right arm. The tiny black dot showed up.

"You marked her?" Lizzie lifted both eyebrows in surprise.

"Well, we had to do something," said Mel. "Even Rosie said she had trouble telling them apart except when they're sleeping. Annie brings her right hand up to her face. Ava brings up the left."

"Well, let's try this again." Lizzie handed the baby to Jace. "This is Annie. Annie, this is your Uncle Jace and he's a really good guy."

Jace looked down.

The baby looked up. She squirmed into a more upright position in his arms, then squinted at him. Her right hand reached up and touched his cheek and his face. And then she patted his face with that sweet baby hand and gurgled up at him.

"She's talking to you." Lizzie grinned. "Look at that, Mel. She's talking to Jace!"

Annie looked around, then back at him. She

frowned slightly, then touched his cheek again and laughed.

"She likes you."

He met Melonie's gaze across the room. "I think she finds me an interesting specimen at the moment. They're pretty little things, aren't they?"

"Beautiful. And this one—" she eased up, out of the chair "—is sound asleep. Should we put her in bed? Hold her? What do we do next?"

Rosie came up the front steps just then, carrying two bags. "Don't let her sleep now, or she'll keep you up tonight. Except that once Ava's asleep, she does not want to waken, so good luck with that." She smiled as she said the words, then set down the bags. "What do we do if Valencia comes back? How do we handle this?" she asked. She faced Jace. "The women filled me in on your story. What if your half sister returns? Do we simply allow her to take these babies, knowing she abandoned them once? Should we call the authorities?" Concern deepened her voice. "I can't understand such behavior because the preciousness of life is very important to me. But what do I do if Valencia comes to my door when I'm watching the girls?"

Jace looked down at Annie. She dimpled up at him, then yawned.

He shifted his attention to Mel and Ava. Then

he sighed. "I don't know. We'll have to figure that out. I'm prone to putting things in the Good Lord's hands, but we need to put their safety first. And that might cause a ruckus if she comes back. Rosie, I have no idea what to tell you."

"Do you think she'll come back, Rosie?" Melonie asked. The thought of someone abandoning this sleeping baby gutted her, because parents weren't supposed to abandon their children. Ever.

Uncertainty clouded Rosie's eyes. "I do not know. She is not a maternal person, and yet I feel she loves these babies. In her own way."

"Maybe loves them enough to give them up." Mel kept her voice soft as Ava squirmed in her arms.

Jace turned her way. "Giving up children shows them love?" Disbelief marked his voice and his expression. "I don't buy that. Caring for kids. Feeding them, clothing them, teaching them. That's what love's all about. Anyone can toss something away. It takes a real parent to go the distance."

He knew nothing, Melonie decided. Because she'd been on the other side of that equation and he was wrong. So wrong.

She stood and handed Ava to Rosie. "I've got to get my stuff settled in the stable."

She walked out, refusing to go toe-to-toe with

him. The only reason she held back was because he'd been handed a rough reality a few hours before.

By Jace's definition, her father had gone the distance.

Wrong.

He'd provided funds to raise her and her two sisters, he'd paid Corrie to mother them and he'd encouraged them to make the grade in good schools. The recent corporate bankruptcy had left her and Lizzie jobless at a time when print media was shrinking. Her father's personal finances had left her and Charlotte with massive college loans to repay. Jobless with massive debt wasn't how she'd expected to face the year, but her late uncle's legacy would help.

As she crossed the sunlit lawn dividing the two arms of the horse stables, she was glad she'd kept silent inside. If tomorrow's meeting went all right, she'd be working with Jace daily. She'd avoid arguments if she could, but she knew one thing for certain: it took a whole lot more than providing food and shelter to be a parent.

No way was he going to take on Gilda Hardaway's job, Jace decided as he steered his truck toward the Payette forest the next afternoon.

He couldn't bring himself to use the term *grandmother*. She'd gotten the title by circumstance only. It might be a biological truth, but it meant nothing to him. And saving her broken-down house meant even less. He was sticking with his plan, one hundred percent. Sell the house. Move to Sun Valley. Take the girls along with him. End of story.

"How'd your night go?" Melonie had been busying herself doing something in her electronic notebook. She looked up as they made a turn. "With the twins?"

"All right."

She whistled softly. "That's not what I heard."

"Well. They're babies. And I know nothing about babies, so let's say it went all right, considering the circumstances."

The twins hadn't loved their new sleeping arrangements. They'd let that be known in full voice several times during the night. Corrie had jumped in to help him, which was a good thing because Jace would have crashed and burned by hour four. This way they both got some sleep. Just not much. The twins woke up babbling and smiling as if they'd gotten a full night's slumber. But then, they got to take naps. Naps didn't happen for grown-ups.

"Were you guys able to get the hay all in?"

"Harve Junior and Wick stayed out late to beat the rain. It's done."

The rain had held off until just after midnight,

but it was coming down now. Not a massive storm. A steady gray drizzle, the kind of rain that benefited crops but thwarted farmers needing to access fields.

But the hay was safe. The girls were with Rosie and Corrie. Now, if he could get through this afternoon's interview...

"And you spoke with your sister?"

Justine. He'd told her as gently as he could, but when she burst into tears, he half wanted to cry with her. He didn't, because big brothers hang strong. Always. "She was shocked. Understandably."

"I expect she was. Whoa." Melonie stretched up in her seat as they took the weed-edged asphalt drive leading up to Hardaway Ranch. Tucked behind trees leading to the national forest, he'd never had a clear look at this house. He'd heard of it, of course. Small towns loved to talk about their eccentrics, and Gilda fit the bill.

But as they emerged from the final curve and the once-grandiose home rose up before them, he took a deep breath.

"Did you just get a horror-film vibe?" Melonie whispered. "Because I sure did."

He couldn't fault her comment because the large, moldy two-and-a-half-story structure would have done Stephen King proud. Surrounded by a yard in desperate need of a brush hog, the place sat like a haunted house on a hill, shrouded by three decades of shrub and tree growth. It was an absolute mess from top to bottom. So bad that he was almost tempted to take the job for the challenge it offered, but not stupid enough to do it. "Here we are." He pulled up to vine-choked steps and stopped the truck. He studied the building, then Melonie. "We don't have to get out. We can head right back to the road and go home."

Genuine surprise made her look quizzical. "Not go in? Are you crazy? I just had to turn down a cable TV contract to come here, and that was tough. That makes this an amazing opportunity. I absolutely cannot wait to get inside. Come on." She opened her door. "Let's go."

She wanted the job.

The anticipation in her voice was reflected in her eyes as she climbed out of the truck. That meant he had to climb out of the truck, too.

He did. Then he studied the house, the choked yard and the sprawling acres beyond it.

Somewhere within him he could almost imagine the beauty it had been thirty years ago. Before he was born, he realized.

He fought a sigh. He was all for getting back into the truck when Gilda's voice called down to them. "I'm here. And I'm waiting. And there's a few things folks my age don't do well. Waiting's one of them. Come on, come on, I'm not getting any younger."

The old saying drew his attention. It struck a nerve or a memory or something... He kept quiet and followed Melonie up the stairs.

Full sensory overload.

Melonie cloaked her excitement as she walked into the big house. She paused inside the door to take in the ruination of what should have been a gracious old home. The classic, wide farmhouse stood as a shell of its former self. Moldings had been damaged by water leaks. Some were rotted straight through. Others had simply disintegrated. Plaster showed water damage in multiple rooms on the first floor, which meant the second floor wasn't going to be too pretty because that water came from somewhere. The thought of reclaiming this wreck of a home and showing off her talents was a power boost for Melonie. Getting this job would keep her in Idaho, as required, but she'd be working away from the smell of the horses. Sheep she could deal with. She had no violent history with sheep.

Horses were another story altogether.

"You're quiet. Both of you." Gilda pressed her lips into a thin line. "I don't like it when folks get quiet because that usually means they're scared to say what they think."

Melonie had been jotting a note in her tablet. She raised her eyes without raising her head. "This doesn't scare me, Gilda."

The old woman looked skeptical.

Melonie jotted something else before she continued. "It invigorates me. It's rare that a designer gets the chance to walk in and lay out a fresh canvas."

"What does that mean?"

Jace shifted his attention to her, too. She'd seen his initial reaction as he walked into the house. Horror...and interest. And something else. Regret, maybe. As if the decay made him sad.

She stopped making notes and faced them. "It means I'm mentally planning massive demolition and starting new. I think the bones of the house are great."

"Bones?"

"The structure," she explained. "The water leaks have done significant damage. The first order of business will be new roofs. Once that's done we can begin the demo inside. No sense starting anything until we've got a solid roof in place."

Jace stayed quiet. He'd brought a few simple tools with him. He poked walls for plaster rot and found plenty. The ceilings on the first floor were ruined, except in the front parlor. He noted that into his phone, then laser-measured the house dimensions. As they moved from room to room, the magnitude of what the elderly woman was asking became obvious.

"Mrs. Hardaway." He slipped his phone into the leather pouch on his belt and rubbed a hand to his neck. "I'm going to be honest with you."

"I am not paying for opinions," she told him in a craggy voice. She'd been following them with a bright pink cane. She tapped that cane sharply against the water-stained floor.

"I beg to differ." He kept his tone even. "That's exactly what you asked, and I'm telling you that the cost of refurbishing this place is astronomical. Perhaps—"

"I've got a five-hundred-thousand-dollar budget earmarked for this. How much help can I get for five hundred thousand dollars?"

Jace stopped dead.

So did Melonie because that was some serious money.

Jace stared at Gilda, then scanned the house, then looked at his grandmother again. "All I'm saying is that we could start over. Something more practical. We tear this down and build a well-constructed ranch house on the site. Everything would be bright and new and accessible." He noted the cane with a glance. "That's nothing to take lightly."

Melonie didn't like Jace's suggestion, but she understood his reasoning. An old woman in frail health—what was she doing here all these years, living amid the decay?

She stood there, silent, letting the old woman make the choice as offered. And hoped she opted for a complete renovation.

Jace had to shoot fair and square, even with the rich eccentric who had shaken his world to the rafters the previous day. He'd handle that later. This was different.

He didn't pretend to like her as she gazed around the house, considering his words. Growing up in Shepherd's Crossing, he'd heard all kinds of things, and he was pretty sure no one much liked her, but this wasn't about emotion. It was about common sense. "We could have it done before winter."

A small, cozy rebuild made more sense. He knew it. And he was pretty sure the women knew it, too.

He didn't look at Melonie. She'd be disappointed because he could see her mental wheels spinning as she moved from room to room. But who in their right mind would put that kind of money into—

"I appreciate your suggestion, young man. I know it makes sense and it's an honest man that lays out the truth even if it doesn't pay as well. But I need my home back." Gilda Hardaway locked eyes with him, sorrow in her gaze. "From top to bottom." She gripped her cane hard, and her hand shook with the pressure. "I messed up my time, but I can fix this if God gives me the days and if you'll take the job. It's not about money, son."

He wanted to take offense at the familial term, but he couldn't because she looked too sad and alone to mean anything bad.

"It's about fixing what needs to be fixed. Can you do it?" She turned to include Melonie in the question. "Now that the first hay is in and the winter lambs are off to market?"

She was ranch-savvy. She'd caught him at a good time. They'd have to hire roofers first, and that would give him a couple of weeks to renovate his house to make it safe for the twins. "I can do it."

"But will you?"

There was the crux of the question.

Could he handle this mammoth job, with help, and still make it to Sun Valley as planned? Because as grand as this job was, it was one job and now he had not one, but three mouths to feed. Two babies to raise. And he couldn't even begin to think about the astronomical costs of day care in Sun Valley.

Stop worrying about tomorrow. If the Lord sees fit to take care of the birds of the air and the lilies of the field, He's got you. He's got this.

Jace wasn't so sure, but when he brought his gaze back to Gilda's, something in her eyes, her face...

Something made him say yes.

He was pretty sure he'd regret it. He already did, truth be told, and when Melonie began shooting pictures of each room, he realized something else.

For the next few months they'd be working side by side.

She'd lay out plans and expect him to follow them. Oh, he'd looked at her magazine that morning as research. She liked to plot intricate layouts, but that was for a two-dimensional magazine, where every shot was strategically perfect.

Gutting a place like this was about as three-dimensional—and dirty—as it could get. And the silk-wearing Fitzgerald woman didn't seem like the type to get her hands dirty. Or compromise. Which meant this could be the longest three months of his life.

Then she turned. Met his gaze. Smiled at him.

Something went soft inside him.

He hardened it right back up. No way was he about to let a pretty smile get in his way. Melonie Fitzgerald had *fancy* written all over her.

He'd sworn off fancy a few years ago when he showed up at the church…and his bride was nowhere to be found. That was a punch in the gut for any self-respecting cowboy.

But when they got to the truck and Melonie turned toward him, excitement brightened those gray eyes to liquid silver. Distinctive eyes set in one of the sweetest faces he'd ever seen.

Maintain your distance. You've been nailed by a woman with dreams of stardom once. Don't be stupid a second time.

He wouldn't be stupid. Not again. But with her bright floral scent filling the cab of the truck, Jace didn't fool himself that it would be easy.

Chapter Four

"We need to have a meeting." Melonie scribbled notes into her tablet at a furious pace as Jace drove them back to Pine Ridge Ranch.

"You're here. I'm here. Let's have a meeting."

She angled a wry look his way.

His jaw quirked, just a little. So he might have a sense of humor hidden under layers of angst after all. Good. "Are you doing the roofs?"

"No. Contracting them out. There's a couple of great roofing companies between McCall and Council. I'll get some estimates for the job. People around here are hungry for work, so we should be able to line up someone fairly quickly. How much of your designs are you running by Mrs. Hardaway?"

"I want to put together a package and present it to her. My goal is to keep it true to the structure and history, but make it more modern. Less fuss, more open space, but still classic design."

"It must have been something in its time."

"Did people realize how bad it was getting?" she wondered. "Did they just ignore it?"

"Well, it's Gilda Hardaway, and you've met her. She's always been rich and beyond eccentric since I've been old enough to know she existed. But you can't see the house from the road, the weeds and brush are a turnoff and, other than a few old-timers, I don't think she entertains visitors."

"So this is a huge step forward for her."

He didn't answer.

He stared straight ahead, his jaw tight and his hands firmly clenched on the steering wheel. She changed the subject. "I'll come up with an exterior palette so we can pick roofing materials by the time we head up there tomorrow morning. And I'll work on the design this evening. It won't be quick." The fact that she couldn't redo a two-and-a-half-story house in a matter of hours made her feel like she should apologize. "I'll need some time."

"We've got as much time as the roofing takes."

"That might not be enough, even if I don't sleep. How about this, instead?" He glanced her way as they turned into the Pine Ridge Ranch driveway, and she had to remind herself that those big brown eyes were off-limits. This guy had "Welcome to Idaho" written all over him. She was headed south once her year was complete. He was staying. "I come up with a quick design for you to fix up your place, you focus on that, roofs get done, my design for Gilda gets done and we move forward in a couple of weeks."

He didn't say anything right away, then he flexed his jaw. "It will have to work."

Have to work?

She climbed out of her side of the truck and shut the door. "'Thanks, Mel, that's a great idea.' 'Glad to help, Jace. Great working with you.'"

She started toward the stables, and it would have been a perfect stomp-off, but then she realized she needed to see his house. Like quickly.

She turned.

He was standing there, stock-still, arms folded, watching her. And a hinted smile softened his jaw and put a sparkle in his eyes. "Forgetting something?"

"You are a particularly annoying person."

"Nothing I haven't heard before." He indicated the house with a tip of his head. "Let's grab sandwiches, head to my place and then you can march off indignantly. Okay?"

"It's not okay at all," she grumbled as they climbed the steps. "It totally loses punch in the delay, so what sane woman wastes a great walk-off when it's already been defeated. No." She turned to face him at the door, and she wasn't afraid to add a slight splash of Southern geniality to her tone. "I will save my stomping for moments of necessity. Right now, we have work to do. You. Me. And my design program."

"So I can expect the cold shoulder at a future time?"

"Only as needed, Jace."

Sassy. Saucy. And strong, despite her diminutive size. Did she know her stuff?

The magazine pictures said yes, but while the pictures looked great, he worried. Did someone have to rein her in and explain bearing walls and structural integrity?

"I smell something amazing."

"Cookie's beef-and-onion soup."

"Be still my heart." She set her bags onto the couch and inhaled deeply. "Who'd have thought soup would smell so amazing on a summer's day?"

"Cookie makes soup all year round, don't you?" Jace asked as they entered the kitchen. "Are we too early?"

"Give me fifteen," answered the cook. "Bread's in the oven. Nothing like hot beef-and-onion soup with fresh-baked bread. There's sandwich makings in the fridge."

"I'm waiting on soup," Melonie declared.

"I'll call the roofers, see who's available to get on the job quickly."

"Because of the farm timing, right?"

He turned slightly. "Because I'm scheduled to leave town by Labor Day and that's already going to have to be delayed with this project."

"You're leaving?"

"Jobs have pretty much dried up around here. I have little choice."

Doubt clouded her features. "But you stand to make a year's worth of money on this project. Correct?"

"That will all depend on costs and labor, but we should both do all right."

"Then why leave now? Why not take the year God's given you and see what happens?"

Just what he needed, a stranger pointing out the flaws in his logic—logic that had worked until yesterday, when he discovered his whole life was a lie.

"I don't mean to interfere."

He was pretty sure that's exactly what she meant.

"But to become an instant father, tackle a huge project and have your moving time delayed until winter, why not put it on hold? Unless you're precontracted there?"

"I'm not."

She faced him, waiting, then she turned.

He hated that she was right, but it did make sense. He'd have plenty to live on with Gilda's project, and using that as a showcase in his portfolio would make sense during the next building season. "I'll add the Realtor to my list of calls."

She grabbed a cookie from the old-fashioned cookie jar that had a place of honor on the counter. Then she paused, grabbed two more and handed them to him as she went back to the living room for her tablet. "Best appetizers ever."

He made the first calls and wasn't sure what soothed him more, getting the roofers to meet him at Gilda's place tomorrow, canceling the sale of his house, or the two macadamia-nut, white-chocolate-chip cookies.

It almost didn't even matter that she was right. He could relist the house if he regretted the decision, but renovating his house while prospective buyers were coming through would be a lost cause. He only wished he'd thought of it first.

He called Rosie quickly. "How are the girls doing?"

"Fine, as always, so adorable these two and getting busy! Ava is determined to walk, but, of course, that means falling."

"You let them fall?" Babies weren't supposed to fall. Were they?

"I blame this on gravity, Jace. Not ineptitude."

"No, of course, I didn't mean…"

She laughed. "I must go—Annie is crawling faster than her sister is walking along the sofa's edge and she seems determined to trip her."

Sibling rivalry already?

He put off the next roofing call to hop online and order three how-to-raise-your-child books. Then he called two more roofers for scheduled meetings at Hardaway Ranch. He might be in over his head when it came to raising babies, but he knew building and he knew ranching. And with three books slated to be here in two days' time, he'd have a firm handle on raising children, too.

"Soup's on!" Cookie jangled the porch bell. Midday meals were casual. Cookie knew folks couldn't just drop what they were doing and run to the house in the middle of the workday.

Suppertime wasn't formal, but it was more structured. At least it had been. With the arrival of the Fitzgerald sisters, new foals dropping, Annie and Ava staying in the big house temporarily and Rosie's infant daughter, Jo Jo, the plethora of small people meant change. Flexibility. And a mountain of diapers, he'd realized yesterday.

He went inside. And saw Melonie busily making notes into her device. She looked up when the door smacked shut behind him.

She smiled.

Those eyes...like mercury.

Mercury's poisonous, in case you've forgotten.

He knew that, but there wasn't one hint of poison in those pretty gray eyes. "Any luck on roofing estimates?" she asked.

"Two can meet me tomorrow."

"Us?"

"Sure, if you want to be there. But it's roofing," he continued. "Pretty cut-and-dried if you're keeping the original lines."

"I'll come anyway. I like being involved in every step of the process—it gives me the feel for the end product."

"Nine thirty and ten thirty. Then a third one in two days, if needed."

"Got it." She jotted it into her online calendar and stood. "Food. Then your place."

Did she think bossy was cute? It wasn't. But when he let her walk in front of him toward the kitchen, he realized she wasn't just cute...she was beautiful. And curvy. And smelled great.

Doomed.

Except he couldn't allow that to happen, so he focused on the delicious food as Melonie put a bit of the melted provolone onto the bread. "This is to die for, isn't it?"

It was but when she had a second helping, he was perplexed. "How can you eat all that?"

She gazed down at the soup, then up at him. "I honestly don't know. Trucker's appetite. And I don't sit around worrying about being a size zero because I like food. And exercise. And last I knew, women were supposed to have curves."

What was he supposed to say to that? "My sister was on a too-skinny kick for a while. It got better, then we lost Mom after Dad died and she slipped downhill again. I hate that she's over in Seattle, where I can't boss her around. Make her eat doughnuts."

"Weight and eating disorders are tough." She sipped water, and frowned. "We humans are hard to figure out at times, aren't we?"

After what he'd found out yesterday? "Can't argue that."

"How hard do you think that was for her?" She stood up to clear her dishes, and he appreciated the effort. Some folks thought Cookie was part maid and housekeeper. He wasn't, but it was nice that she didn't have to be schooled on ranch manners. "Your grandmother, I mean. To come here like that and tell you everything?"

"Not as hard as it was on me hearing it." He didn't soften the bitter edge of his voice. He stood, too, then raised his hands. "Sorry. This isn't your fight, and twenty-four hours isn't enough time for me to be waving the peace flag."

"I wonder when it will be time?" she said softly, and when she walked toward the kitchen, he realized she might not be talking about him. "Cookie, that was the best. Thank you so much for making it. I wouldn't have thought hot soup would taste so good on a beautiful summer's day."

"You're welcome. Jace said you two are heading to his place to figure things out. You might want to grab a few of those." He indicated the cookies with a glance. "His cupboards are pretty bare. He makes sure the horses have food. He doesn't worry so much about himself."

"The few times I eat at home don't require a lot of groceries." Jace grabbed his cowboy hat from the wall of hooks just inside the back door. "Although if I'm up at Hardaway's place and raising two little girls, I'll have to change that up pretty quick."

"Truth." Cookie liked to wear an old-style fishing cap in the house. He said it was to keep hair out of the food, but Jace figured the older man just liked wearing a hat. The cook raised one finger to the hat as they were leaving. "See you at supper."

Melonie grabbed her two bags. He held the

screen door open for her and tried to ignore the sweet scent that came back to him as she went by.

"You have horses?" she asked once they were settled in the truck.

"Two," he answered. "Sometimes I keep them at Pine Ridge. We used to take the sheep into the hills for browsing but we had to stop doing that."

She arched one really well-groomed eyebrow in silent question.

"Government changed up the rules and took away grazing rights."

"Lizzie said something about that but we didn't have time to go into detail. So now the sheep are pretty much being raised in the valley?"

"With more hay, less exercise so less muscle mass."

"Oh, of course. That makes sense."

Now he was the questioner. "You get that?"

"We had fresh-raised turkeys in Kentucky. It was a Fitzgerald thing. We only raised enough for family and friends or esteemed business acquaintances of my grandfather. It was a mark of acceptance to be given a Fitzgerald turkey in November."

"And this relates to sheep...how?"

She laughed. "Good point. When you eat a store-bought turkey, the consistency is different. It's been tenderized. The home-raised turkeys had a much firmer feel."

"That's it exactly." He sent her an approving look. "The sheep will be the same weight and look the same, but the ratio of fat to lean will be slightly different and the texture will vary. Here we are," he said as he pulled into the driveway. "That's Bonnie Lass over there." He pointed to a dark sorrel mare on the far side of the split-rail paddock. "And the black-and-white is Bubba. My dad's horse. Would you like to go see them?"

"No."

He'd started that way. He stopped, surprised.

She took a step back and shook her head. "I can admire them from afar, thanks. Lizzie and Char are the horsewomen in the family. I'm better inside a house than inside a barn."

How did someone with an aversion to animals just become quarter owner of a multimillion-dollar ranching operation? "Good to know." He moved back and led the way to the front of the house. He unlocked the door and waited for her to follow.

She didn't.

She stepped back and snapped several pictures of the exterior.

"The outside doesn't need fixing."

She jotted something into the tablet and

shrugged. "I want to envision the whole package, if that's okay? Just like with Gilda's place."

She followed him inside.

He expected criticism because the real estate agent had given him a hefty list of changes—a list he tore up as soon as she was gone.

Melonie surprised him instantly when she grabbed hold of his arm. "Jace, this is charming."

"Is it?" He ran a hand over the stubble along his jaw.

"Well, it needs a little spruce-up, some painting and some crown molding, but look at these built-ins." She motioned to the floor-to-ceiling bookcases flanking the fireplace. "You put a wood-burning insert in here."

"The Realtor told me I should pull it out and redo the fireplace. She said it adds eye appeal to the buyer."

"And then they freeze all winter?" When she rounded her eyes in disbelief, a wave of relief washed over him. "Cold winds, slashing rains, heavy snow? Who wouldn't want a cozy wood-burning stove to come home to?"

"Exactly. It takes the pressure off the heating bill and gave me some extra money to help Justine get through college."

"Jace, what a good brother you are." She'd been jotting quick notes as she moved through the downstairs rooms. Now she turned. Met his gaze. And then she didn't stop meeting his gaze. She brought one hand up, her free one, and touched her throat.

Oh, man.

He wanted to step forward. Smile at her. Maybe flirt, just a little.

He stepped back instead. "There are two bedrooms and a bathroom upstairs."

"Let's check them out." He followed her up the stairs. She paused at the top and snapped a couple of pictures. She didn't say anything.

That kind of unnerved him. A quiet woman was a rare bird in his experience, and as she tapped things into her tablet, he shoved his hands into his pockets. Then pulled them out again. He motioned downstairs. "I can make coffee. I've got a one-cup system so it's always ready."

"Coffee sounds great," she told him. But she didn't look up. She was perched against the short stair rail at the top of the stairs while her fingers flew.

"Okay." He went downstairs. Made the coffee. When she didn't come down, he called up to her. "Coffee's ready."

"Perfect."

She hurried down the stairs, and came really close to sliding across the hardwoods like he'd done as a kid. "Is it in the kitchen?"

"On the counter. There's milk, too. And sugar. Nothing fancy, though. Sorry."

"Black's fine. If it's great coffee, why ruin it with all that other stuff?" She grabbed the coffee, took a seat at the table and sipped. Then she savored the moment, eyes round, before she lifted the mug like a salute. "Perfect blend."

"Cowboy blend," he told her.

"You made this?" That got her full attention. "Like the actual coffee beans and stuff?"

"No." He didn't sit. Not in the middle of the workday. There was too much stuff to do. "I order it from a place in Boise—White Cloud Coffee. This is one of their signature blends. Cowboy."

She smiled at him, then took another sip of pure appreciation. "It's ideal. Not bitter. Not weak. Great aroma."

"You love coffee." He did, too. Maybe too much.

"I love good coffee," she corrected him. "I will admit to being a coffee snob. It's a fault, I know."

"Then it's one I share because bad coffee shouldn't be allowed."

"Exactly." She smiled up at him again. Did she know how inviting that was? Was she using that pretty smile to break him down before she gave him bad news about the house?

"I'm going to go take care of the horses while you nose around, all right?"

She lifted the ironstone mug. "I've got coffee in a great mug and the info I need. I'm good."

"And cookies," he reminded her. He set the little pack of Pine Ridge cookies on the table. "It's like afternoon tea, ranch-style."

"Way better," she told him.

He went outside, conflicted.

She dressed upscale and talked hometown-friendly. Until she turned the drawl on to put him in his place.

He smiled, thinking of that, then stopped smiling because he was thinking of it. Thinking of her. That's all he needed, to fall for another woman with big dreams of TV or stardom or anything that wasn't down-home Idaho.

His phone buzzed a text from Justine. Can we talk? Soon? Because I can't get my head around all this, Jace.

Him, either, but he was older. Call me tonight.

Busy now?

Getting house ready for babies.

Unbelievable…but cool. In a weird way. Coming home in a week to meet them. Hug you. Figure things out.

She needed to touch base with reality, just like him. Good. Can't wait to see you. Talk later.

He finished filling the water trough, then opened the grain bin.

Both horses headed his way. Bonnie trotted the length of the paddock, still spritely at ten years old.

Bubba plodded along, an easygoing old fellow. He wouldn't last much longer, most likely. He was ancient in horse years. He snorted toward Jace, spattering him. "Thanks, old man."

The aged gelding nodded as if pleased, then went to his grain bucket.

"A man and his horses."

He turned, surprised to hear her voice. "I thought you didn't like horses?"

"I have enough respect for them to keep my distance," she told him. "They're over there. I'm here." She pointed to her side of the fence. "It's all good. I've got some quick ideas to show you."

"Already?" He stroked his hand along Bubba's neck, reminded the horses to behave, then came her way. "That's quick."

"I kept it basic," she told him as they walked back to the house. "What you could do, what you should do and what must be done. Then I'll work up the design specs on it tonight so you can jump in."

"More coffee?" he asked her once they were inside. He kicked off his boots at the side entry.

"Your mama raised you right, cowboy." She flicked a glance at the boots. "Barn boots don't belong inside."

Your mama.

Funny how a simple term like that had felt so good two days ago. Now it cut deep because he'd found out she wasn't his mother.

Oh, she loved him. Jace had no doubt about that. Ivy Middleton had taught high-school science, raised two great kids and kept a sharp eye on their small holding and his father. She doted on faith and family, one hundred percent.

But she wasn't his mother after all.

"Please say that dark expression isn't heading my way."

He grimaced and pulled up a chair once his coffee was done brewing. "Sorry."

"The adoption thing has you spinning."

He glared at her for being right, but it wasn't her fault so he made a rueful face. "It's like a weight on my shoulders. Not that they adopted me, because they were the best parents anyone could ask for. If you wanted model parents, Jason and Ivy Middleton were the benchmark."

"Ivy?" Her eyes went wide again. "Oh, I love that name." She sighed softly. "It's so pretty. I love that old-fashioned names are coming back in style." She placed her right hand over her heart. "Dignity and beauty comes with the name."

"That was Mom. But she hated lies. She was honest all the time, so why keep this a secret? It's not as if folks don't adopt children all the time."

"Good questions with no answers you want to hear, I expect."

"Grandparents are raising grandkids all over the country. But not mine. Because I didn't fit the image of a Hardaway grandson."

"Their loss. And not for nothing, cowboy..." She sat back and sipped her fresh cup of coffee. "If they were as mean-spirited as Gilda made herself out to be, they did you a huge favor. I'd be writing her a thank-you note."

He started to glare, but paused when she raised her hand.

"You ended up without any of the negative nonsense that was so prevalent thirty years ago. That's all I meant. How is your sister handling this? Justine, right?"

"She's calling me later. Wants to talk. And she's coming home next week. She's in the middle of an internship in Seattle, and probably can't afford the time, but she wants to see me. Meet the babies. And come to terms with all this. But I'm not sure how to help her do that when I hardly come to terms with it myself."

Chapter Five

Melonie wasn't exactly an expert on forgiveness. Her father had given her more than enough experience with untrustworthy relatives, but she hadn't reconciled any of it. She probably needed to get over the urge to do a full-fledged father-daughter smackdown first, an urge that went against what she believed. What her faith taught her. She frowned. "They say time is the best help. And faith. But in my experience, it hasn't exactly worked like that so I'm no help. Sorry."

"Lizzie said your dad messed you guys over." He ran one finger around the rim of his mug, frowning. "That's got to be rough. I'm sorry you ladies had to go through that."

"Us and a few thousand employees when he embezzled all the corporate funds he could get his hands on." She pretended a bright smile. "And now he and his current significant other are lolling in Dubai, spending other people's money. But here's a lovely and quite notable difference." She opened her notebook and pitched him a smile. "Your parents loved you to distraction. My sweet mama went home to God when my sister Charlotte was a baby. I was a toddler. We never knew her. We have no memories of her, just photographs.

"We had Corrie," she continued. "She called us her babies and she meant it. So we didn't have a mother, not much of what you'd call a father and our grandparents were caught up in Kennedy-esque dreams.

"Through it all we had Corrie. She was there at every event, every recital, every soccer game, every choir practice. And that's what I mean about Gilda doing you a favor, because if it had been my dad in the stands, things would have been quite different. Because no matter how well you did, it was never going to be good enough." She slid a list across the table. "Here's my rundown. Must. Should. Could."

"I organize my jobs and seasons that way." Approval laced his tone. He read the list. "Yes to the must list, and to the should column as well. Why not do it all right now while the roofers give me time?"

"That was my thought, too." She waited a few beats. "And the could list?"

"To pretty up the outside?"

"Yes."

She wasn't asking for the moon, and if he did revisit selling for the following spring, the house would be ready. "Yes."

"All right. Are you fine if we keep the outside classic, like it is? This isn't a historic landmark, but I'd like to keep the historic look. No new siding. The clapboard is perfect, it just needs painting. Vintage-style shutters. Paint the picket fence, which I love, by the way. New gutters. Wash and paint the concrete porch. And we'll pretty up the gardens."

"I meant to keep them up better." He gripped his mug with both hands. "But then there wasn't time. They were my mom's gardens and she had a sweet hand with them."

"I can see it."

He looked skeptical for good reason. To an undeveloped eye the landscaping was a mess.

She laughed. "I really can, despite the weeds and the old stems poking up through. There are tricks to keeping things tidy now, with little or no weeding. Leave it to me."

"I'm not used to that." He met her gaze frankly and she had to fight the little catch in her throat when he did that. "Handing over the reins on personal things."

"Pretend it's professional."

"Except that we're talking about my house. My home. My parents' house," he added softly, and there was no denying the longing in his tone. A man who loved and missed his parents.

"I'm giving you veto rights," she told him.

"Yeah?"

"Sure. I'll have the design set by morning because we're not doing anything major. The house is wonderful as is. If this was a car, we'd call this a detail job."

"You don't want to change the kitchen cabinets?"

She stared at him, then the classic cabinetry, then him again. "Only a fool would mess with something like that. Do you want new cabinets?" It pained her to even think of these old beauties being taken down.

"No, but the real estate agent suggested a full tear-out. She said the kitchen update should be at the top of the list."

"Agreed. But we can work *with* the pretty cabinets. Not against them. The very idea is ludicrous." She stood and took her mug to the sink. "We should switch out the sink and the countertop and do a fresh paint job. And a new light fixture. Then change the appliances as you need to, but watch for sales."

"Easy enough."

"We're in a time crunch. Here, give me your mug, I'll rinse it out for you." She put out her hand.

So did he.

Her hand closed over his on the mug. Then she looked up. Met his gaze.

Eyes the color of rich cocoa with just enough gold flecks to brighten when he smiled. Thick eyebrows. A firm jaw. Corrie told her once that a good man didn't blubber or fuss or fumble much with words. That a good man had a strong heart, well-set shoulders and a firm jaw.

This cowboy fit the definition to the max.

His eyes swept her face. Her mouth.

Then he let go of the mug, withdrew his hand and stepped back. "You can just leave it."

She rinsed it anyway, and set it on a dish rack to dry. A meow sounded outside the door.

"Barn cat. Great mouser. I'll make sure she's got food before we go."

"I'll meet you outside."

She gathered her notepad and camera bag. And her purse. When she walked through the side door, he was waiting.

"My mother loved this little covered entry."

"Quaint and picturesque."

"She called it a proper entry for an old home."

Melonie's heart melted. "She's right. So many old places became add-a-room houses. It's not easy to do additions that keep the integrity of an old place while addressing necessities."

"What made you decide to do this?" he asked as they walked to his truck. He didn't walk real close to her, but not all that far away, either. "Designing? Homes? Making things pretty?"

"See, that's the common misconception," she told him once she'd pulled herself up into the truck's cab and snapped her seat belt into place. "Function first. Unless I'm working with someone who absolutely doesn't care about function and the sky's the limit. But for us normal folk, it's about function. Make it accessible, safe, keep the flow of people in mind and then make it pretty enough so no one feels engineered."

He backed the truck around and headed for the road.

"My grandmother was the inspiration for our design magazine," she explained. "She loved to see a home come back to life. Not as a profession, but she had an eye for how to make it work. When my sisters were out winning equestrian events, I was designing floor space with graph paper and a pencil. Once I discovered computer-aided drawing, the rest was history. I could create, change, practice and never have to waste another sheet of paper."

"Do you need my help tonight?"

"Are we picking up Annie and Ava now?"

He nodded.

"Then, no. You spend time with those babies so they get to know you. I'll work in the stable apartment."

"Your uncle put a great office on the first floor," he reminded her as he turned into the Pine Ridge Ranch driveway.

"And it's lovely," she said smoothly. "But I like that full flight of stairs between me and the horses. And that apartment is crazy cozy."

"Will you stay out there when Heath and Lizzie get married?"

"An Independence Day wedding and a back-yard barbecue reception, two things that I might not have associated with 'Fitzgerald wedding.'" She laughed as he swung the truck into Rosie's driveway. Two small shepherd homes stood side by side along the longer ranch driveway. Aldo lived in one, and Harve and Rosie lived in the other, with their kids. "We'll see. Charlotte's good with animals, your house should be ready for the girls by then, and it might make sense for Char to take the stable apartment."

"The house will be ready." He'd pulled off his cowboy hat and tossed it behind the back seat of the truck. "What about me?"

"One big, strong cowboy and two baby girls? How hard can it be?" She smiled at him, teasing, and moved to the door.

* * *

He found out how hard it could be that night. Annie was teething.

He didn't even know what that meant until Corrie rubbed some sort of salve on the little girl's gums and gave her a pain reliever. "Just rock her," she told him. "Once it takes the edge off, she'll probably go back to sleep."

Her and him both, he hoped.

"Would you like me to do it?" she asked.

He'd love it, but it wasn't Corrie's responsibility. It was his. "Gotta learn, right?"

"And experience is the best of teachers."

He settled into the wide easy chair and rocked the little one. She fussed at first, scowled up at him, withdrew the bottle, put it back, then scowled again. Like it was his fault. Or maybe she was just downright mad that he couldn't make the pain stop instantly. He was kind of mad about that, too.

She struggled to sit up.

He tried to keep her lying down in his arms.

She frowned again, sat up and gave him a trucker's belch.

He stared at her in disbelief.

She patted his cheek, then pulled the bottle back to her mouth with one hand. The other hand played with the wisps of hair along her cheeks, then slowly, rhythmically, she began twisting a tiny hank of hair with her finger.

Sleep stole up on her like a summer sunset. Nothing hurried about it. And when she finally closed her eyes one last time—and the bottle went lax in her mouth—he stared at the absolute miracle he held in his arms.

So small. So dependent. So perfectly beautiful.

Blond wisps framed her face, a face that seemed more pale against his darker hands. Black lashes lay against rounded cheeks. A tiny nose. A little mouth. And not too much chin to speak of, yet.

She wasn't a year old. That meant at least seventeen years of parenting.

She frowned as if the pain was coming back.

He shifted back in the reclining rocker and started humming.

She settled her pretty little head against his T-shirt, sighed and dozed off again.

So did he, and he didn't feel a thing until they both woke up nearly five hours later.

Ava had woken up. She'd come to the side of her portable crib, spotted them and started babbling something very loud and pretty funny because the little blonde kept making herself laugh.

She reached out, patted his knee, then tugged her sister's leg.

"Sissy is sleeping," he told her. "She had a rough night."

"Bah, bah, bah, bah, bah!" Ava insisted, tugging at Annie's bare leg again. "Bah!"

One man.

Two babies.

One sleeping.

One not sleeping.

And him, caught in the middle. Did he dare try to put Annie down? Would she wake up? Did it matter?

He started to move but the door opened softly. Melonie slipped in and reached for Ava. "I've got her," she whispered.

Ava instantly grabbed two hands full of Melonie's gorgeous dark curls. And then she pulled.

"Hey, baby, that's not how this is supposed to go down." Melonie loosened one of Ava's hands. "You've got a great grip, kid," she added as she unwound the second hand.

Ava's face went sour.

Her lower lip came out.

By the time Melonie got her out of the room, she'd let out a full-fledged wail that grew fainter as Melonie went down the stairs.

How would he manage? How could he possibly do this if he just utterly failed his first test?

Corrie came into the room just then. "Here." She eased the still-sleeping baby from his arms.

"Let me tuck her into her bed—that probably wasn't the best night's sleep you've ever had, Jace."

"Compared to cold, hard ground when we're running sheep, I'd say this chair and a sleepy baby were all right. I smell coffee."

"Cookie's got the kitchen ready for action."

He stood and stretched, then watched as Corrie bent low to set Annie into the crib.

He raised an eyebrow when she straightened, and she motioned him out the door, then spoke. "Babies fear falling. If you go down with them, cradling them, it's not scary. It's just plain nice."

"And you kind of kept your hand on her back while she settled."

"Too quick, they wake up. Patience and time are your biggest assets. And a sense of humor."

Her words made him smile. They also made him question.

Could he handle this? Raising two precious children?

He turned the corner at the bottom of the stairs, and paused.

Melonie was tucked along the corner of the couch, feet out, cooing to Ava as she gave her a bottle.

Ava's tiny hand kept patting Melonie's dark curls, as if she was happy to see them. Feel them. Touch them. And when she began to knit her hands into Melonie's hair, Melonie scolded, "Uh-uh. Don't do it, missy."

The baby let the bottle go loose and giggled.

Then she wound her fingers in Melonie's hair again.

Another scolding.

Another giggle. Louder this time.

That baby not only understood Melonie, but she'd also turned it into a game.

"Are babies that smart?"

His voice surprised Melonie. She turned quickly. The strap of her tank top slid off her shoulder, just a bit, letting her dark hair fan the lightly tanned skin.

She shrugged the strap into place, made a face at Ava, then him, and laughed. "Seems like it. So how are we going to stay two steps ahead of you and your sister, Miss Ava? Because I expect that will be quite a job."

"A juggling act."

Melonie made a face. "It's all in the timing. And sleep deprivation," she added, smiling.

She was beautiful in the morning.

Beautiful at night.

An at-ease kind of beauty that seemed like it was part of her.

She didn't flirt with him.

He grunted at Cookie, poured coffee and kind

of wished she would because he wanted to flirt right back.

He shouldn't.

No, make that couldn't. He'd learned his lesson and he understood her goals. She'd practically prebooked her flight back to Kentucky and her cable TV dreams once her year on the ranch was up.

Once burned, twice shy.

But when he went back to the living room, carrying coffee for both of them, the sound of her voice, laughing at that baby…

The joy in her voice made him wish she was laughing at him like that, and they were only on day three. How would he manage to keep his distance for the next several months?

Chapter Six

"Oh, thank you." She gave him a grateful look when he set the mug of coffee on the table. "I stayed up to get the basics done on your house, so this coffee will become my mainstay for the day."

"And Annie is teething, according to Corrie."

"Does that mean you held her all night?" The look on her face made him feel like a hero. He wasn't a hero. He was just a guy with a job to do. Three jobs, he realized as he took his first long sip of coffee. Two precious girls, helping on the ranch and now an unexpected mega construction contract on Hardaway Ranch. Was it only a few days ago he was hoping for a job to fall in his lap? Yep.

He set down the mug. "It kept her happy."

"Oh, Jace."

She lifted her eyebrows and offered a sympathetic smile. "That is so wonderfully kind of you."

"Yeah, well." He scrubbed a hand to the back of his neck. He needed a shower. And a shave. Probably a haircut, too.

"My dad used to do that with Justine," he told her. "When she was sick. I must have been like six or seven years old. He'd hold her and rock her and she'd fall asleep in his arms. And when I'd get up in the morning, he'd still be there, in that big old rocking chair, holding his baby girl."

He'd glanced away, picturing the image. When he brought his gaze back to hers, there was no missing the sheen of tears in her eyes.

Her eyes glistened.

He reacted instantly.

"Hey. I didn't mean to make you cry. Stop that," he told her. He grabbed tissues from a side table. Since Lizzie had come to live on the ranch, tissues had appeared in almost every room. A woman thing, he guessed. "Here."

"Don't mind me, I get sentimental way too easily, but what a perfect memory, Jace. And what a lovely portrait of your family you've given me."

"They were wonderful." He shrugged. "I only wish I'd told them that more often. I should have made sure they understood how special they were."

"They knew."

He looked up.

"By the kind of man you are. By the beautiful daughter who cares about others. It's not the words that matter, Jace. It's the actions, and you and your sister have shown that again and again. Especially now." She dropped her gaze to little Ava.

The baby tossed her bottle aside, burped and giggled.

"She's not like a *baby* baby, is she? They're almost more like little people now. In diapers."

"Speaking of which." She swung her legs over the side of the couch.

Then she began to stand.

Ava reached for the coffee mug.

Jace jumped forward. He grabbed the baby's arm just before she snatched the mug of hot coffee, and there he was, right there, almost cheek-to-cheek with Melonie, and the tiny trouble-seeking blonde between them.

"Great save. I couldn't dodge backward quickly enough."

"And this time it was two-on-one," he told her. "Upstairs it was one-on-two until you came along. Right now I'm thinking the odds are against me."

"'If God be for us, who can be against us?'" Melonie quoted Paul's verse to the Romans gently. "Parents have been raising multiples forever. It's just that most of them have nine months to prepare, physically and mentally. You got an hour."

The common sense of her words struck him. "You're right."

"Oh, Jace. *Darling*." She handed Ava to him and smiled, teasing him with the meaningless drawled endearment. And then she drawled the rest of the words, sending his pulse sky-high. "You will find out that I am almost always right."

Heath and Zeke came in from outside just in time to hear Melonie's comment. "While they don't look alike, that is one thing these sisters have in common. They are both *almost* always—" Heath stressed the word almost with intent deliberation "—right. A fact that bears getting used to. Hey, dollface." He plucked Ava out of Jace's arms. "I expect you want a shower," Heath said to him.

"The world around me would certainly appreciate it."

"Zeke and I will take baby detail. He's been like a big brother to these two girls since they were born. He'll coach me along. Won't you, big guy?" Heath clapped a hand onto Zeke's five-year-old shoulder as they crossed into the dining room.

"I know everything they like and don't like,"

bragged the boy. "And all their best foods. Mostly Rosie still feeds 'em stuff. But just mostly."

"I believe our young friend here is telling us that while finger foods have their place, these little ladies still like to be waited on." Corrie followed them into the dining room with two bowls of something. She thrust one at Melonie before handing the second one to Jace. "Most nutrition still comes from the spoon or the bottle. I put baby spoons with each. When they are done eating, I will pack them into the stroller and walk down to Rosie's with them. If that's fine with you, Jace?"

He stared at how quickly Annie began devouring whatever was in the bowl. "It's wonderful. What's in this bowl and why does she like it so much? Because it looks dreadful."

Corrie laughed. "Rice cereal, mashed banana and vanilla-flavored Greek yogurt. A full meal in a dish."

"Ava loves it, too."

"All my babies loved this," Corrie told them as she fixed herself a fresh cup of coffee. "Simple good food, high in nutrition and calories that babies need."

"They need calories?" Jace didn't mask his surprise. "Aren't they already on the fat side?"

Corrie stopped moving.

Heath took a long step back.

Melonie stayed absolutely quiet because she was thinking the exact same thing.

Corrie tsk-tsked Jace. "These are perfectly normal, healthy babies. They are not fat," she assured him. "They are exactly as they should be. If you had been held and fed for nearly ten months, how would you look?"

"Like a barrel?" he suggested.

"Yes. Both babies will soon be walking. Then running. Then climbing. They will barely stop to eat and you'll be scratching your head, thinking they're starving themselves."

"Corrie, for real?" Melonie squeezed Ava's chunky little calf and the baby giggled.

"Nature's way is amazing. It prepares them. And then they keep us running for a long, long time." Corrie aimed a fond look at Zeke. "Little boys sporting casts are just one prime example of how adventurous life becomes."

"I'll hang on better next time I climb a big tree," boasted Zeke. "Dad says they'll take my cast off really soon, then I can play in the water. Or swim in the creek with Dad!" The funny boy raised his casted arm like a badge of honor.

Memories washed over Melonie. Her hands refused to move.

Broken bones.

A broken face. A wired jaw.

Long days of pain in the hospital. Long weeks of liquid food and more pain.

Then the first glimpse in the mirror, of her bruised and battered eight-year-old face. She'd gone off to hide, almost wishing the horse had done her in.

Corrie found her like that. Held her. Whispered to her. Let her cry. And then Corrie went to their hometown library and brought back pictures of people who'd had their faces wired.

And they all looked normal and wonderful and good.

For the first time since being pummeled by hooves, hope had chased fear aside. It came back as she healed, but in the end, Corrie had been right. As usual.

"Did you hear me, Melonie?"

She swung around as Jace came closer. "Sorry. No. I was focused on mush, I guess."

Corrie aimed a look her way from the other side of the pass-through. A look of love and understanding, and maybe a little concern.

"If you bring your notes for my house along this morning, we can swing by the lumberyard this side of McCall and get everything we need."

"I'll show you the plans once the girls are on their way to Rosie's with Corrie, all right?"

He paused by her chair, nuzzled Ava's round, pink cheek and made the little girl giggle out loud. "Yes. Give me an hour in the barn with the guys, then time to shower. Heath said they could use an extra pair of hands."

"An hour works for me." She tried not to notice how good he smelled because ignoring his good looks was impossible enough. The complete package was harder yet. He rolled his shoulders as he moved away.

She bit back a sigh and turned her attention to Ava. "You're done," she exclaimed a few minutes later. "You did great, Ava!"

The baby burbled up at her, lifted her eyebrows and grinned.

"They couldn't be cuter, could they?" Lizzie lifted Annie and washed her little face and hands. "Mel, do you have time tonight to go over wedding plans with me?"

"I will make time. I'm a wretched sister for taking this amazing job on when I should be helping you plan barbecue."

Lizzie laughed as she gently cleaned Annie's little face. "Scoff if you will, but people around here take barbecue seriously. Not as seriously as Texas or the deep South."

The truth in that made Melonie grin.

"I know this job is important to you," Lizzie continued. "We're having most of the food catered so folks don't have to worry about anything. But you have an eye for placement, and putting things together. I want it to look nice without messing my equine budget."

"It's amazing what I can do with clean Mason jars, wildflowers and two dozen lace tablecloths."

"I love lace tablecloths." Lizzie patted her heart, Southern girl to the max. "I wish Charlotte was here to help plan."

"Me, too. But she'll be here in time for the wedding. And then for at least a year."

Lizzie handed the soft, warm washcloth through the pass-through. "We might have to sneak away tonight so we can plan things."

"Why?"

Lizzie raised one of those perfect Fitzgerald eyebrows her way before she slanted a look toward the door. "These men are a distraction."

"Oh, Heath. Of course." Determined not to blush, Melonie trained her gaze on the baby.

"Not just Heath."

"Lizzie. Stop."

Her sister laughed as she took the baby up the stairs. "I'm going to get clean clothes for each of them. Corrie, can Zeke walk to Rosie's with you?"

"He surely can, and we might just stay and play for a while if he'd like. Or he can walk back here and help in the barn."

"Like all by myself?" Zeke hollered from the front porch. "From Rosie's?"

"Will you stay out of the way of tractors and cars?" Corrie phrased the question like only a really silly person would get in the way of either.

Zeke mashed his face against the screened wooden door. "Cross my heart."

"Then, sure, why not? Last time I looked, this place is going to have your name on it one day. Might as well learn early what owning a big spread is about. Taking charge. Getting things done."

Zeke's eyes rounded. "And I can be a big cowboy like my dad!" He dashed down the steps, climbed onto the hitching-post rail across the way and brandished a pretend lasso over his head with his good arm.

By the time Corrie had the girls packed up, Jace was heading their way. "I'll let you two go over plans." Lizzie moved toward the equine barns west of the house. "You know where to find me if you need me."

Jace held up his watch. "Do we still have time to look things over before we meet the roofers?"

"Ten minutes is all I need. Would you like to look at things here or at the table?"

"Here's fine." He kicked off his boots at the door and settled alongside her on the couch.

"Can you see the screen?"

He inched closer... He'd been throwing straw. The scent of yellow straw and green hay clung to him.

"Coffee." Cookie came into the living room with to-go cups and set them on the coffee table. "I figured you might be needing some by roofer number two. And pretty sure your grandma doesn't stock cowboy blend."

"Thank you." She smiled up at him.

Jace acknowledged Cookie's statement with a wry look. "True enough. Thanks, Cookie."

The cook tipped one finger to his fishing hat. "No problem."

Focus on the computer. On your work. Ignore the hunky guy sitting right next to you.

"The first floor." She pointed out changes to him, updates that would bring some life back to the house. "I've moved your bedroom upstairs, and shifted your room to an office and this room to your sister's room. If that's all right with her."

He pulled out his phone and texted Justine right away. She answered with a quick thumbs-up emoji. "Done. That way I'm on the same floor as the girls."

"Exactly. Jace, what if this doesn't all get worked out legally? What if their mother comes back and takes them or the county doesn't let you have them?"

"A serious question that deserves a serious answer." He folded his hands in his lap and leaned forward. "It might take months to get things worked out. I expect the county will give us temporary permission to watch the girls when we ask, but in the meantime, I'm just figuring that the girls are visiting their uncle. And their uncle needs to have things ready for them."

"You don't worry that the county might take them away?"

He shook his head. "No, because for all of my grandmother's bluster, her money speaks around here. You see the mess she's made of things. But in their day the Hardaways helped a lot of people. If Gilda Hardaway claims these girls as her great-grandchildren, no one's going to argue, especially when a simple DNA test will bear her out. And if she asks her long-lost grandson to take care of them, no one will blink an eye at that, either. What Gilda says, goes."

"And their mother?"

He stared at her, confounded. "I don't know her. I know she's abandoned them once, and that Rosie and Harve Senior had concerns about her. I can't predict the future."

She nodded.

"But I can prepare for it the best I'm able. Either raising two precious little girls or putting up a new For Sale sign next spring."

"You don't worry?"

"Try not to," he told her. "My parents didn't believe in worrying. They believed God would provide. And that the rough roads of life built character. I always thought I took after them." He slanted a rueful look her way. "Oops."

"Nature might get things started but nurture adds the finishing touches." She flipped to the upstairs layout. "I don't know where we girls would be without Corrie. She's the only mother I've known. It didn't matter that she didn't birth us. It mattered that she loved us. And she's been right there with us, every step of the way, even when the money ran out."

"Selfless love."

"Yes."

"I like that you're going to put a full bath downstairs. It'll make life easier with kids."

"And it could make prospective buyers happy."

He stood quickly. Was it her changes that caused that swift response? Or the thought of selling the family homestead? "Gotta grab that shower and hit the road."

"One more thing." She flipped to the home's exterior page, then held up the layout image for him to see.

His expression changed. He sat right back down. Then he reached out one finger and traced the outline of the stone-rimmed garden beneath the bedroom windows. "You can do this?"

His face was filled with love and longing and something indefinably sweet. "Yes."

"It's perfect." He indicated the picket fence separating the house from the road. "I should have kept that up better. I knew it. Then the weather bested me and I couldn't make it a priority."

"Now you can. We don't want the girls to get splinters."

"No, of course not. I—" He braced his hands together, then faced her. "I don't know how to thank you."

She started to shake her head, but she stopped when he laid one strong, calloused hand against her knee. "Don't shrug it off. When that Realtor started on me to change this and do that and fix the other thing, all I heard was take apart your whole life, throw it away and buy plastic."

She half smiled, half winced. "Ouch."

"I couldn't do it. It was like doing demo on our lives. But this." He faced her directly. "This is beautiful. My parents would have loved this. Simple beauty." He met her gaze and then, for long, drawn-out seconds, he kept meeting her gaze. As if wondering...

She was wondering the same thing, but she was only here temporarily. She hadn't come to take over the equine side of the ranch, like Lizzie had done. She wasn't here to make her mark on western Idaho. She was here to claim the stake her late uncle offered. A share of an enterprise. Then someone would buy her out, she'd return to civilization and continue her quest for a nationally renowned cable TV show.

She closed the laptop, stood and grabbed her coffee and her notebook bag. "I'll be in the truck when you're ready to go."

Her phone buzzed a text as she climbed into his truck a few minutes later. She opened it. Production company didn't just like the mock episode, Ezra informed her. They LOVED it. Time crunch is a problem. Call me.

So the production company loved it, but there was no getting around the time crunch. She was here for the coming year. Despite that, the news made her smile.

"Good news?" Jace asked as he took the driver's seat. He turned the key and thrust the truck into gear. It jerked, then stalled. He started it again, then scolded the engine. "Hang on until I get the first third of Mrs. Hardaway's money, okay? I'm not draining the savings account to save your sorry hide."

"Nice news, yes," she answered. She motioned to her car parked next to the three-stall garage. "I had no idea how expensive car repairs were until our family fell apart. Talk about a reality check. It's like a thousand here, a thousand there."

"I'm good around a lot of things, but new engines aren't one of them. Now, an old tractor like that one." He pointed to the big green rig near the sheep barn. "That's a tinker's dream. One part comes off. The other one goes on. With some coaxing along the way. Not a circuit board in sight."

"You like working on vehicles?"

"Winter work," he told her. "Your uncle heated the far barn so that we can overhaul equipment all winter, get it all ready for spring."

"I cannot even imagine what it would take to heat a place that size for the whole winter."

"Do that again."

She frowned. "Do what again?"

"The drawl."

She was tempted to go all Southern belle on him, but that would be stupid. And after having her last boyfriend walk out when he realized she was broke and in debt, she wasn't about to mess around.

Her goals didn't include life up north, so she refused the invitation to flirt. "I worked real hard to lose the drawl for mass-market appeal. The irony is that if I get my own TV show—" she faced him more squarely "—they're probably going to want the drawl. So the joke's on me."

He didn't respond.

He stared straight ahead while one finger tapped the steering wheel lightly.

He might not think much of her goals, but she'd grown used to that with her father and she knew one thing for certain. No way was she going to live in the shadow of someone's chronic disapproval ever again.

Chapter Seven

Jace's spine went stiff when she mentioned television. "The magazine stuff wasn't enough for you?"

"It made a great stepping stone. But TV was always the dream."

Her words hit him like a dash of ice water on a mid-July day. "Everyone should have a dream." He'd said the words, and mostly he believed them. But he'd been there before with a fame-loving woman and wasn't about to make that mistake again.

"Agreed."

He pulled into his grandmother's yard. The first roofer's truck had pulled in just ahead of him.

He hopped out and shook the man's hand, then introduced Melonie, and when they went up the steps, he let Melonie pick which side she'd go up…

And he chose the other with the roofer squarely in between. He'd been left cold once. He understood women and their weird mix of feelings and the lure of dreams. He might get it…but he was never going to let it affect him again. No matter how enticing the drawl was.

By the time they'd met with both roofers, it was lunchtime. Gilda met them by what had once been an ascending garden. Now it was a heap of towering weeds and thin trees trying to stake a claim in the hillside soil. She came forward with a purposeful stride, the four-pronged cane smacking the ground with each step. "Are you hungry?"

He started to shake his head but Melonie replied first. "Starved. What's the plan?"

"I've got fresh bread and peanut butter and some of Sally Ann's good jam. She works down at the Carrington Ranch and she makes the best jam around, though no one says a word of that to Millie Gruber. She's a sensitive sort and folks worry about her feelings." She peered over her glasses at them. "Let's talk roofing."

Jace followed the two women, wondering what happened to the you-make-the-decisions-and-I'll-sign-the-checks mentality.

He didn't want to eat in the wretched house.

He didn't want to eat with this old woman who cast out children, then grandchildren, as if they were unwanted commodities. But he couldn't very well leave Melonie here, and she was already up the back steps.

A cat yowled.

He stopped dead, imagining cats on counters. On tables. Roaming around the sprawling house.

But then the cat dashed out from beneath a huge yucca plant, over toward the old barn.

The barn had a solid roof. He was just thinking how odd it was to reroof the empty barn and ignore the house when the door squeaked open. "Coming?"

He faced Melonie.

He wanted to back away. The combination of the broken house and broken lives was too much. How one thing affected the next and then the next until a twisted network of lies and half-truths knotted itself. He was just about to say no when she held out a hand.

Just that.

Her expression stayed calm, but her eyes and that hand said she understood.

He moved forward when every fiber of his being wanted to go the other way, and when he climbed the four wide steps feeling grumpy and probably looking worse, she winked at him.

Not flirting.

Just…understanding.

The wink broke the mood.

If a formerly rich Kentucky girl could handle eating in the decaying mansion, he could, too.

He followed her inside.

"I forgot how to do fancy and nice a long time ago," said Gilda as she moved about the room with more comfort than she displayed outside. "But a clean sheet's as good as a tablecloth and the food's fresh."

She'd spread a bright floral sheet over the table. Jars of fresh peanut butter and homemade jam were placed like centerpieces. A loaf of bread sat to their right, and a pitcher of tea stood to the left. "This is lovely, Gilda," Melonie said.

The old woman rolled her eyes, but acknowledged the antique rose-covered pitcher. "I got the tea recipe from your magazine. I'm not much for trying new things, least I didn't used to be, but it looked good and tasted better. When I heard you were coming to town, and other things started falling apart, I realized maybe there's a reason for the tea recipe. And the magazine. Your sister's got a good heart," she went on as she handed them knives for the peanut butter and jam. "She didn't mind stopping by and sharing her ideas for getting things going. I didn't think much of it initially, of course."

Jace was pretty sure that was accurate.

"I like my own ideas in my own time…"

Another spot-on self-assessment.

"But when you don't necessarily have much time left, you start listening better. When I heard the preacher's words at Sean Fitzgerald's memorial service, I thought to myself 'Old woman! You'd best get going if you're ever going to make a difference in the world.' A good one, that is." Her hand paused. Her face shadowed. And for a brief moment, Jace almost felt sorry for her.

But not quite.

"So you decided to start fixing things?" Melonie asked. And then she did the nicest thing. She'd spread peanut butter across her slice of bread—peanut butter that managed to fill the kitchen with a familiar nutty fragrance—and she handed it to him.

He started to refuse it. "I can do my own, Melonie." But he stopped when she gave him that look again. A look that pushed him to go along with the kind gesture. "Actually, thank you. That's nice of you."

He spread jam onto the peanut butter, topped it with another slice of textured wheat bread, and when he took his first bite, the mix of flavors seemed like old times at his mother's table, feasting on PB&J.

"I didn't used to like simple." Gilda didn't put peanut butter on her bread. Just jam. "I thought too much of myself to even think simple, and that's the shame of it. I look back and shake a fist at myself, sayin', 'Gilda, what were you thinkin'?' And yet I know exactly what I was thinkin', being a woman who thought herself above others. That's the devil's own way of it," she told them, almost scolding. "No matter how your life goes, or what wonders come your way, you don't want to get caught in that kind of a cycle. It's wrong, and while a part of me knew it then, I kept right on. Now, your mother..." She pointed her bread at Jace with an adamant expression on her face. "Ivy Middleton was one of the best women I've ever met, and I should have told her that more often but we were afraid of gettin' up talk. Having folks figure things out. Because then you'd know things and the last thing she or your dad wanted was for you to be the talk of the town."

"So how exactly did they explain the sudden appearance of a one-year-old baby?" he asked point-blank. "Because if talk was what you wanted to avoid, handing over a baby in a small town probably wasn't the best way to do it."

"There's talk and then there's *talk*," she told him frankly. "She told folks that God had brought them the miracle they'd been praying for all along and folks loved her enough to let it go at that. Not being able to have children was a sorrow for so many, so when Justine came along six years later, that was quite the surprise and the joy, I'm sure."

He loved being Justine's big brother. He'd loved helping his dad with her when Mom was working.

"I'm not expecting you to love me, Jason."

He'd been about to eat the last corner of the sandwich.

He didn't.

"I don't expect anything of the kind from anyone, but I have this vision," she told him, then included Melonie in her look. "Of this house bein' a home like it's never been before. Like it's never had a chance to be. With kids running up and down the hill. Playground stuff, too, like swings and slides and the stuff that childhood should be made of. Not stuffy gardens and fancy furniture like before, but a home. The way things should have been all along. I want to see it be that home before I die." She coughed then. Not too loud and not too long, but enough for Jace to understand.

"You wanted to discuss the roof," he said, changing the subject.

"I do not, I just figured it might be the only way to get you into the house and tell you my goals." She nailed him with a look. "You looked ready to jump ship. I don't have time or energy to chase you down, and there's no one else I want to do this job, so if you're having second thoughts, tell me now."

He sighed. Put his head in his hands for just a moment, then peered at her. "I was having second thoughts. But I gave my word, and a man's word is his bond. I won't let my reluctance mess this up. And I'll do a great job. But I can't just throw emotion away. I expect you know that."

"I do. Nor do I expect you to let bygones be bygones. It's too much to ask, of course."

It wasn't.

It was exactly what his faith told him to do. What kind of person would he be to ignore that?

"But I will be ever grateful for the help, Jason."

He wanted to correct her. He was named for his father, but everyone called him Jace. For as long as he could remember.

But oddly it sounded right from her. He stood. "Thank you for lunch."

"Thank you for staying."

"It was delightful." Melonie stood, too, but she reached over and hugged the old woman.

Jace didn't. He headed to the door. "I had another roofer appointment lined up for tomorrow, but I'm going to cancel it. Melonie and I both liked the second appointment today—"

"Western Idaho Roofing."

"Yes. Good prices, great reputation and quick start date."

"Do I need to leave the house?" Gilda asked. Jace frowned.

Melonie got the gist more quickly. "You should be fine, but it will be noisy, Gilda. Why don't you come over to Pine Ridge during the day until it's done? It shouldn't take them more than a week. We'd be happy to have you."

"You can tell when someone's new in town, because not too many hand me invites these days," the old woman grumbled, but she looked less grumpy. "I might just do that. I don't do well with a lot of noise."

"Rosie might bring the girls by with Corrie. And her newborn baby. That can get real noisy."

"There's noise and then there's noise, young man, and while I can probably hold my own rockin' a baby, electric air hammers and drills aren't friendly to a woman my age." She faced Melonie more squarely. "I will accept your kind invitation, Melonie."

"Lovely. I'll let the others know." Melonie squeezed her hand gently. "And we'll have tea on the porch in the afternoon."

"Something to look forward to."

He looked Melonie's way when they'd climbed into the cab of his pickup truck. "You've got that sugarcoated, sweet-tea-offering Southern persona down well."

She frowned. "Excuse me?"

"Back there." He gestured as he turned the truck around. "Come to the ranch? Have tea on the porch? That's pure Kentucky, isn't it?"

"Or it's simple kindness to an infirm, elderly woman who's about to embrace a huge undertaking and trusts us to oversee it," she argued mildly. "She's grown old, seen the error of her ways and had a change of heart. Isn't that the basis for some of the best stories? The prodigal son. The woman in the street, about to be stoned. I love stories of redemption."

So did he. But not when the old person's solace came at the cost of his family's joy. How were he and Justine supposed to react to all of this, knowing their parents had woven a web of dishonesty around their lives? "Easy to say when it's not your life being affected."

She made a face, a kind of cute face of self-doubt. "You're right about that because if my father came to beg forgiveness for all his misdeeds, I'd be in a flux. A parent should only be allowed so much latitude. And then they lose the right to call themselves parents."

"Then the same holds true for grandparents."

She shook her head. Was she being intentionally obtuse? Or trying to fluster him? "Advanced age cuts them slack. They were raised in a different way. A different time. We have to be mindful of that. This forest is just gorgeous," she added, smoothly changing the subject. "Like being in the Appalachians, but different, too. Not as many deciduous trees."

"Being this high and this far north changes what grows." He mulled her words as they headed for the lumberyard in McCall, unwilling to let the topic go. "You think the older the person, the more forgiving we should be."

She was tapping notes into her notebook. She paused as he rolled to a stop at a four-way and slanted him a look. "I think we should always be forgiving but I'm about the world's worst example so let's not go there. If I never saw my father again, I'd probably be okay with that, which means I've hardened my heart, mostly for self-preservation. But you." She closed the notebook and set it aside. "You had a wonderful life. A beautiful family. You're so skilled at all the trades your father loved. Ranching. Carpentry. Building. You said yourself that he kept you by his side all along."

He nodded as the home store came into view.

"Gilda might be the worst grandmother ever, but she made sure you had great opportunities. That can't be discounted."

He scowled. "Around these parts, we expect

folks to do what they're supposed to do. All the time." He pulled into the parking lot and shoved the truck into Park before it was fully stopped, making it jerk.

She rolled her eyes. "If we need extra lumber we could always get it from that full-size chip on your shoulder." She slung her purse up, got out, then faced him as they rounded the truck.

"So is that whole sweet, Southern-woman image some kind of joke?" he asked. "Or do we only pull it out for grumpy old ladies?" He folded his arms and stared her down.

Looking up, she met his gaze without wavering and he wished he didn't like her panache. Yet he did. "Clearly you missed *Steel Magnolias* and *Fried Green Tomatoes.*"

She folded her arms, too. "Let me tell you something. This Southern gal is going to help you get that house in order so that you can create a family with those perfectly adorable little girls. Be the father they would never have had if their mother stayed. A father like the one you had, Jace."

Her words hit the mark like a well-balanced nail gun.

She walked toward the store, head high.

A father like he had.

A blessed, wonderful man who showed goodness and kindness all of his days. Strong but loving and forgiving.

He hated that she was right. At some point he'd have to admit that.

He rubbed the nape of his neck as she cruised through that door, wishing she didn't look so good. The way she stood her ground with him made him almost look forward to sparring with her again.

If he wasn't careful he was going to find himself knee-deep in attraction with another unattainable woman, and that couldn't happen. But when he walked through the doors and caught her guarded expression, what he longed to do was make her smile again.

And that was a danger-laden emotion.

"You'll come with me to my bridal fitting tomorrow, won't you?" Lizzie asked Melonie that evening. "If you can tear yourself away from Jace… I mean his project, of course."

Melonie purposely ignored her sister's intentional gaffe. "Yes, if you guys don't mind dropping me off at his place on the way back. As much fun as this all is—" she swept the busy ranch yard and house a quick look "—it's not quiet enough for me to design what I need for Gilda's place, and I've got two weeks to get my overall plan in order. By then, Jace should be done with his house and we can dive into the Hardaway place. But I'm going to need every minute of focus I can get."

"You think construction is quiet?"

Melonie laughed. "I can work upstairs while he's remodeling the first floor. The sound of tools won't bother me, but kids, people, doors banging, horses... I'd be distracted."

"I think you're going to be somewhat distracted at Jace's place, too, but what do I know?" Lizzie ducked away from the couch pillow Melonie flung at her, then grinned. "We'll be happy to drop you off after the fitting."

"Perfect." It wasn't exactly perfect because Lizzie was right. Avoiding Jace would be in her best interests, and yet...she didn't want to. And she was grown up enough to keep things under wraps because as cool as Pine Ridge Ranch was, it wasn't exactly quiet. Unless she hid out in the small apartment, and being that close to huge horses wasn't about to make the short list. "I can't wait to see you in the dress."

Lizzie sighed. "Me, either. Can you believe it? Us here and me about to be married to the love of my life?"

"I heard that, which means you want something." Heath braced himself with one arm on the side of the wooden screen door, then jerked his head. "Come walking with me. Let's see what that first full moon of summer holds."

"I'd walk in the moon's light with you anytime, cowboy."

Melonie stuck out her tongue at them. "Go, lovebirds. Some of us have work to do."

Heath opened the door. As Lizzie stepped through, he leaned down for a kiss...then took her hand, leading her into the moonlit yard looking so utterly in love that Melonie's heart wanted to break into a million little lonely pieces.

"Please tell me that angst isn't directed at me."

Jace's voice surprised her. He must have come down the back stairs. She dipped her chin toward the laptop, choking back emotion and biting back tears. "No angst. Just getting ideas down."

She felt him watching her.

She hoped he'd go outside or back to the kitchen. He'd been tucking the girls into bed with Corrie, and the whole process had taken a long time.

He didn't leave.

He moved her way. "Are the plan ideas giving you a rough time? I might be able to help." He took a seat across from her and when she drew her gaze up, he seemed genuinely concerned. "I'm no designer but I'm good at knowing what will and won't work if you've hit a bad spot."

"It's not the design aspects."

He frowned, then followed her gaze to where Lizzie and Heath had paused for yet another kiss. "Ah."

Her forehead knitted instantly. "Ah, nothing."

"Hey." He splayed his hands and shifted his eyebrows up, intentionally dubious. "I find the whole thing annoying, too. Happy people, planning their lives. What is the matter with them?"

"Stop. You're not helping." He was, though. Laughing at the situation was way better than crying over being dumped by a ladder-climbing young executive back in Louisville.

"You're talking to a man who got left at the altar."

Now she stared at him because she couldn't begin to imagine that.

"True story. It was not my best day."

What a wretched thing to do to anyone, and the idea that it happened to him seemed outrageous. "Then the girl was clearly stupid and not meant for you, because what woman in their right mind would do that, Jace?"

He laughed. "My thoughts exactly, but she did and it took me months of embarrassment to figure out she did me a favor." He jutted his chin toward the ranch yard. "I watched Heath lose his wife and struggle with a newborn baby, a full-time job here on the ranch and grief. It wasn't pretty and there was nothing I could do to help my best friend. And when Camryn left me at the altar, he tried to help, but there's not much other folks can do. Except be patient. Be kind. And praying's never a bad choice."

"I'm getting closer to that whole did-me-a-favor mind-set," she confessed. "When my family's publishing company was closed down, my job was gone and I had a bunch of debt ascribed to me by the courts. My ex wanted no part of that."

"So he *did* do you a favor. He didn't deserve you."

"Well…"

"No arguing," he scoffed. "It's fact. If a man isn't smart enough to love you for yourself, who needs him?"

It sounded so right coming from him. "So we're the walking wounded?"

"My scars are healed, but I am most assuredly gun-shy," he said firmly. "Between your uncle's illness and the ranch, we've been so busy the past couple of years that it didn't much matter."

"The shortage of women might have made them easier to avoid," she noted, smiling.

"Shortage of people in general, which spurred lost job opportunities here." He stood and rolled his shoulders, easing kinks, and she tried to pretend he didn't look absolutely amazing when he did it. "Now with kids to raise, my focus needs to be on them."

"Agreed." She stood, too.

He stayed right there, looking at her.

She looked right back.

"So why is my focus longing to shift, Melonie?" He whispered the words as he gazed at her. Her lips. Then her eyes. Then her lips again.

A half step forward. That's all it would take to see... To test this attraction. It was a half step she didn't dare take. "Stop that."

He smiled. Raised one hand to her cheek. The feel of his palm, so strong. So tough. So rugged. As if she could nestle the curve of her face into his hand, his shoulder and stay there...forever?

Her phone rang.

She took that half step then, in the opposite direction. "You." She pointed at him, scolding. "I don't play games. Take your crazy cute cowboy self out of here so I can work." She tapped the phone to take the call, as if talking to her newly graduated veterinarian sister back in New York was vital. "Hi, yes, it's Melonie, may I put you on hold for just a moment?"

Jace left.

But he left whistling, his hands loose at his sides, as if Charlotte wasn't the only thing put on hold. Maybe she should hole up in the equine apartment to work, after all. "Char, thanks. I just had to finish a meeting with a client."

"You've been there a few days and already you have clients? Color me surprised."

"There are plenty of surprises out here, believe me. When are you coming?"

"Not for two weeks. I'm following up on a few horses here and my reciprocity paperwork should allow me to open my mobile veterinary practice there by mid-July."

"I know that's the plan, but there aren't a lot of people here," Melonie told her. "There might not be much actual work."

"Then I'll consider every little bit a blessing. I can't get large animal experience without hanging a shingle. How'd you snag a client so quickly?"

Melonie filled her in.

Charlotte sighed. "This whole crazy family dynamic seems to be epidemic, doesn't it? What's up with that?"

"I don't know." Melonie tucked her toes beneath a throw pillow as the evening temperatures dipped. "I see the mistakes in all of it, but Jace—he's the cowboy construction guy—ended up with the nicest family. Great parents. He loves his sister. So maybe she did him a favor, after all?"

Charlotte stayed quiet for a moment. Then she partially agreed. "Maybe. That's a fairly Pollyannaish outlook, isn't it?"

"I love Pollyanna."

Charlotte laughed. "I know you do. I just think that while it's nice to be optimistic, it's good to be on your guard, too. Like twenty-four/seven. Three hundred and sixty-five days."

"How'd you get so jaded for such a young person?"

"Twenty-six isn't all that young. And my plans for living a bucolic life in some posh Southern practice where little old ladies dote on their puppies have been dashed, so bear with me."

"You'd die of boredom and you know it. You're the adventurer among us. And you actually like big animals."

"Love 'em. So this crash course on an upstate New York big animal practice has been good for me. And downright dirty. Overalls and muck boots are my new wardrobe."

Melonie laughed as Jace came into view again. He and a couple of the men were talking in the yard, gesturing toward the hills, the hayfield, the pastures. When Lady came up alongside, seeking attention, Jace didn't think twice. He reached down, still talking, and gave the former stray dog a good petting.

"Just as well. The little old ladies out here are a breed apart."

Charlotte laughed. "That must make Corrie happy."

"Let's just say she's not one of a kind in the rugged north."

"Oops, gotta go—a call out from a farm and it's late here. Hope they've got decent lighting."

Melonie ended the call and set down the phone.

She needed to dive into the broad scheme for Mrs. Hardaway's house. She needed—

The men began walking away.

Jace spotted her watching. And for long, slow ticks of the living room clock, they locked eyes again.

Was his heart skipping beats like hers? Were his palms growing damp?

Stop this. You know better. You know your plans. You're leaving here as soon as you've secured your inheritance. His life is here. Yours isn't. And there are two baby girls to consider.

Her conscience delivered the wake-up call she needed. She wasn't here for a rebound romance. She was here to help the ranch and if the Good Lord saw fit to toss a possibly career-changing job into her lap, so be it. She'd had to leave her chance once. She wasn't going to mess it up a second time.

She shifted her attention back to the computer. She needed to keep things all business with Jace, and avoid those sweet baby girls, even if their big blue eyes and winsome smiles called to her.

They had Corrie and Rosie to mind them. And Jace. With a big job before her, she could keep the babies with the more experienced women. The hard part would be keeping all three of them—Jace and those little girls—at an emotional distance.

Chapter Eight

"Melonie gave you a list?" Heath grinned as Jace loaded garden tools into the bed of his pickup truck the next morning. When he tossed in two rolls of landscape fabric, Heath's smile stretched wider. "Pretty domestic for just meeting the girl, isn't it?"

"All part of the makeover," Jace replied smoothly. He aimed a stern look Heath's way. "Are you helping me demolish those two walls or not?"

"Getting to use a sledgehammer and wreck stuff?" Heath flexed. "I'm all in. And this is way more fun than I'd anticipated before a certain Fitzgerald sister rolled into town. Wearing silk, I might add."

Melonie and her fancy pants. No one around here wore fancy pants like that. He might actually hate them if she didn't look so good in them. "Do you think she even owns blue jeans?"

"Well, we know she's got leggings." Heath tipped his gaze to the three women, moving toward the ranch SUV parked next to Jace's truck.

Jace had tried not to notice, but when someone looked as good as Melonie Fitzgerald, only a blind man would be immune. "You gals heading to Boise?"

"There's a shortage of wedding-gown seamstresses around here, so yes." It was Lizzie who answered. Melonie stayed quiet on the opposite side of the vehicle. "Mel said you guys are tearing down two walls today?"

Heath flexed again, making the women laugh. "We've got this. They dropped off the Dumpster yesterday afternoon. We're on a mission."

"You remember which two walls, right?" Melonie asked.

"I hope so," teased Jace. "You might want to stop by and mark them with an *X* so we don't mess this up."

She looked like she wanted to smile.

She didn't.

She gave a polite wave as she opened the car door. "I'll see you two in a few hours. And don't forget the garden stakes, okay?"

"In the bed of the truck as we speak."

"Perfect."

When he and Heath climbed into the truck, Heath laughed. "Man, have you got your work cut out for you."

Jace deliberately misunderstood. "Getting the Hardaway roof done is buying me time. Once my reno is complete, I can move the girls home. Then I tackle the monster-sized project." He waited until the women pulled away, then followed them up the long driveway.

"I was talking about your partner. The one tapping things into that notebook in the car up ahead. Does she ever stop working?"

She'd told him she was ambitious and nothing he'd seen so far negated that. "Doesn't look like it."

Heath studied the car ahead, then Jace, but he stayed quiet. And by the time they'd gotten the two walls down and the debris into the Dumpster, Jace was pretty sure he'd just made the biggest mistake of his life. His mother's house—her lovely, historic home—was now filled with plaster dust and gaping holes where walls had been.

Sure, he knew they'd fix it. But it still felt wrong.

"You men are amazing!" Lizzie's voice rang with approval as she stepped in the back door just after one o'clock.

"Oh, this will be a fine piece of work," Corrie chimed in as she entered. Could they see beyond the mess to the finished product? Right now he couldn't.

Melonie came in last. She didn't look at what they'd demolished. The part of his past they'd just destroyed.

She looked at him. Just him. And when she gave him a nod of approval, it helped. She set a big bag on the counter and studied the newly opened layout. "With the support beam here." She pointed up. "And the beautiful wainscoting, this will keep all the historic flavor we want but open things up for the girls to see and be seen." She turned her attention up to him and the sincerity in her cloudy gray eyes did another number on his pulse. "You guys did a great job."

Then she smiled. Not a flirting smile. A smile of such understanding that he wanted to hug her. Thank her. Because for a minute there, he was pretty sure he was wrecking something precious. He wasn't. He was changing things for something precious. Two somethings. He moved to the wall nearest them. "I know you wanted a closet here, but what about if we move the closet there—" he pointed to the left "—and keep this wall for kid pictures?"

"Kid pictures?" she asked, puzzled. "Won't you just put them all over?"

He shoved his hands into his pockets. Rocked back on his heels. "I thought it might be cool to keep putting pics up there. As they grow. To show all the changes in what they do. Who they are and who they turn out to be."

Her mouth formed a perfect O. "I love that idea. A wall-of-progress kind of thing—that's brilliant, Jace. What made you think of it?"

He shrugged and pulled his hands out of his pockets, almost nervous. But he never got nervous, so why would he be anxious now? "Just something I've thought of. Having a family someday. Seeing kids grow. Having all that cool stuff up on a wall."

"It is a wonderful idea, and it will be a beautiful balance of old and new," offered Corrie.

"Are you all set here?" Lizzie asked Heath. "If you need to stay, I can come back for you later."

"My part's done." Heath raised his hands in surrender. "The fixin' part is up to Jace. What are you two doing for lunch, though?" he asked Melonie and Jace. "There's no food here."

Melonie pointed to the counter. "We stopped by Shy Simon's in Council. I got us a Triple S pizza to share. I hope that's all right."

"A meat-lovin' cowboy's dream," he told her as Heath, Lizzie and Corrie headed out. He didn't want to smile at her, but he had to. She wasn't afraid to take charge. To make decisions. To move forward. He wasn't stupid, he knew that those same qualities would take her away next year, but what if she had reason to stay? What if staying became more important than leaving?

Dude. Been there. Done that. Disastrous results, remember?

She grabbed a bag and went upstairs quickly, the way she did most everything.

There was plenty to focus on without letting romantic nonsense mess him up. And there wasn't a place on an Idaho ranch for a woman who feared dirt. Dirt and hard work formed the backbone of Idaho. They went hand in hand.

He'd just convinced himself that Melonie's outfits put her completely out of the running when she dashed down the steps wearing loose capris, a faded T-shirt and a bandanna around the dark waves of her hair.

He stopped. Stared.

She looked at him, then herself, then back at him. "What's wrong? What did I do?"

He gestured. "The outfit."

She frowned. "Like it? Hate it? The yard won't care," she suggested with a quizzical expression. "I'm doing the front gardens today."

"*You're* doing them?" He couldn't hide his surprise because that was about the last thing he expected to hear. "I thought you were working on the Hardaway project and I'd get to the gardens as I could."

"I did work on the project," she told him. "All

the way to Boise and back." The drawl crept back into her tone as she talked. The drawl that he found crazy attractive. "I wasn't about to waste valuable hours when I could make some significant progress...which I did," she added.

She walked over to the pizza, selected a slice and a paper towel, and went straight out that front door after she grabbed a hat that came right out of the pages of a Southern ladies magazine. Then ate her slice of pizza while surveying the yard.

He wanted to go talk to her.

He didn't.

He'd unloaded the tools from the bed of the truck and lined them up beneath the cluster of catalpa trees his grandmother planted over forty years before. His adoptive grandmother, he realized.

He hated the new adjectives in his life. He'd been fine without them. Fine without knowing a truth that was kept from him. And fine with the house the way it was.

His phone chimed a text from Rosie. He opened the message and the picture she'd sent widened his grumpy old heart.

Annie and Ava, both standing, laughing, clutching the edge of Rosie's sofa and proud of their newfound freedom. The video clicked to life.

Annie shrieked in glee. Ava joined her. Then

Annie released her death grip on the couch. She reached out and clutched her sister in a hug.

Ava hugged her back, and their faces…filled with laughter, the image of innocence, bright with joy.

He swallowed the lump of grouchiness that had taken hold a few days before. His parents weren't here to explain their choices, but that shouldn't matter. They were part of him. They'd raised him. Taught him. If they felt the need for privacy about the adoption, maybe it was for good reason.

"Jace? Do you have any old pictures of your mother's garden? In color?"

He was the worst person on the planet when it came to finding old stuff. "Probably in a bin somewhere."

She laughed.

His heart gentled. He strode forward and opened the door. "I could hunt them down," he told her as he took the three steps down to her level. "But maybe it would be nice to plant some new stuff. Create some new memories for the girls."

"A great idea." She focused on the shovel, then paused. "Then you're all right if I remove some things? I don't want to get rid of something cherished."

"We need to have a few roses," he told her.

"Mom loved her roses but they'd get nasty every time we got a rainy stretch."

"We can plant a few disease-resistant varieties," she told him. "They don't get blighted easily. But I'd like to keep that climbing rose on the trellis," she continued. "If it gets too spotty, we can replace it next spring."

"Mom's favorite. She loved that grayish pink. Said it reminded her of old British novels." He reached over and lifted a shovel.

She turned, surprised. "I've got this. You've got inside work to do. I need to do something physical after being in the car. It clears my brain."

"It's supposed to rain tomorrow, so the more we get done out here today, the better. I'll start over here." He moved to one corner of the front garden. "How about you start at that end and we meet in the middle?"

"Sounds goods."

As they tossed old plants into the wheelbarrow, the clean smell of fresh dirt motivated him.

She didn't talk while she worked. Neither did he. He tried to ignore her, but when she started humming vintage dance tunes, she made it impossible.

Music.

He grabbed his phone and hit the music app.

She turned to him, surprised. "Nobody likes old music like that anymore. Except me."

"And me." He set the phone on the stack of black mulch chips. "Glenn Miller. Frank Sinatra. Nat King Cole."

"I used to pick old songs for my dance routines growing up," she told him as she worked his way. "The other kids thought I was crazy, but it got me two dance scholarships."

He whistled lightly. "You must be good."

"Well, it's like kittens. Or a litter of puppies," she continued. "If you have three orange kittens and one gray, the gray will get picked to go to a new home first. Because it's distinctive. Not better. Not worse. Different."

"Now you're negating the merit of your efforts." He frowned at her. "Don't do that. Nobody hands out scholarships because the music stands out, Melonie. They hand them out because the dancer stands out."

She looked at him.

He looked back. Suddenly Sinatra's "The Way You Look Tonight" started playing.

Jace put out his hand. She studied the hand, then him.

Then she laid hers in his.

It didn't matter that their hands were dirty. It didn't matter that hers were small and narrow and his were big and broad.

They fit.

And when he led her onto the short grass and spun her into a twirl...

She laughed, and it was about the prettiest sound he'd ever heard.

"You dance." She smiled up at him as he drew her back in.

"I love to dance. With the right person, of course." He slanted a knowing look her way.

She blushed and batted him on the shoulder. "No flirting allowed."

"But dancing's all right?" He laughed as he kept the moves in time with the music across the yard and around the thick-leafed catalpa trees. As the song drew to a close, he did a quick turn and dipped her. There she was, snug against his arm, head back. Her dark waves of hair cascaded over his arm.

"Dancing is always all right," she whispered, gazing up at him.

His heart caught, midbeat, because the feel of her there, in his arms, was so right. "You are beautiful, woman." He smiled down at her.

She smiled back.

Close. So close. Close enough to imagine leaning in for a kiss.

Was she wondering the same thing?

It didn't matter. They both knew better. And they had work to do.

He drew her back up until she was steady on her feet. "Thank you for the dance."

"My pleasure, sir."

Her slight curtsy made his heart tumble a little more.

Just then, his phone rang.

He crossed to answer it, then frowned. "We've got to go. Zeke and Annie have both come down with some kind of illness and they can't be around Rosie's baby. We'll have to keep the kids at the ranch house the next few days."

"Let's put the tools in the garage so they don't get mucked up in the rain."

Her suggestion surprised him. Why would a bunch of garden tools mean more than sick kids? He frowned. "No time. Let's roll. Or I'll send someone back here for you."

Nobody bossed Melonie around. Not now. Not ever again.

She waved a hand. "I'll stay here. You go tend the girls."

He stood still for just a moment. Then he climbed into his truck, backed it around and left.

The jerk.

Not for leaving for a sick kid, but for the Jekyll-and-Hyde maneuver.

She kept working, pulling plants and tossing

them. Then smoothing the ground with the thick-forked rake.

She tried to draw up mental images of the Hardaway house as she worked, but mental images of Jace came up instead. The way he moved. The way he talked. The slow smile.

She didn't dare dwell on how the man danced, or that they loved the same old music.

A bedraggled clutch of coneflowers got to stay.

So did a daisylike flower near the porch, airy and pretty.

She deep-sixed almost everything else except for half-a-dozen primrose plants, long past flowering.

Once she'd laid and pinned the weed barrier, she sliced holes for the current plants, drawing them through. The bits of color popped now, as if they were happy.

A part of her wanted to call and see how the girls and Zeke were doing. Another part needed to maintain distance.

But that was already impossible. Spending a year here in Idaho, working with Jace, watching precious babies grow… That meant she'd have to try harder. When things fell apart, Melonie Fitzgerald simply tried harder. Besides, if something was seriously wrong, Lizzie would've contacted her.

An hour later, Melonie had just finished clearing the second small border garden when Corrie drove in.

"Child, you have your mother's touch with gardens, that's certain," she said once she'd parked the SUV.

"You think?"

Corrie put a hand to her heart as she crossed the yard. "Your sweet mama and I spent a lot of time in the gardens together. We both loved digging in the dirt and growing things. You are the only one to have the eye for this, and that is straight from your mama. It does my heart good to see it."

The thought that she was like the woman she couldn't remember seemed right and wrong. "I've always wished I could remember her."

"I know."

"You'd think that there'd be something, wouldn't you?"

"Memory is a funny thing." Corrie reached down to stroke a daisy blossom. "You might not consciously remember her, but those kindly feelings you shared, when she'd sing you to sleep, or dozed off with you in her arms, made you feel safe and secure. That security is part of who you are today, darling girl. And it started back then. In your mama's arms."

"How's Annie doing?"

"Fussy and feverish," Corrie reported. "I thought I'd come this way and see if I could give you a hand, though. They've got things covered there."

"But what if Ava gets it?"

"Well, that will make things busier."

"Let's not worry about this," Melonie told her. She stripped off the garden gloves and tucked the tools into the garage. "I can work on designs back at the ranch and help with kids if needed."

"You don't want to be getting sick with this big project coming up," Corrie said.

Right now that was the least of her worries. "I've got two weeks before the roofers get their part done, then nearly a year to see it through, Corrie." She closed the garage and slung an arm around Corrie's broad shoulders. "At this point I've got nothing but time, it seems. Let's go check those little ones."

"All right."

Corrie backed the SUV around and headed out the driveway, and by the time they parked alongside Jace's truck, Melonie's phone chimed a text from Lizzie. "Seems Ava's running a fever now, too."

"Then it's good we've got all hands on deck," Corrie told her. "We'll take turns rocking and singing, I expect."

"Like you and my mother did for me. For all of us."

Corrie blessed her with the smile she remembered growing up. The smile of a woman who loved her through thick and thin. "Just like that."

When she got inside, Heath was holding Ava and Zeke was curled up on the far sofa, sound asleep, dark lashes fanning against his milk-chocolate-toned cheeks.

Ava reached for Melonie.

That sweet baby half leaped out of Heath's big, strong arms the moment she spotted her, leaving her no choice.

"Hey, precious." Melonie curled the fussy little girl into her left arm as if she'd been doing this forever instead of scant days. "Hey, hey. I'm so sorry you don't feel good, darling."

"She doesn't want to rock. Or eat. And I just gave her medicine to bring the fever down," Heath told her.

"Well, then maybe a walk outside would be nice? Let's go breathe some lovely summer air, sweetness. I can walk with her out there just as easy as in here."

"That's a good idea. Jace is rocking Annie upstairs."

She took Ava outside.

The change of scene seemed to brighten the baby's mood. She stuck her pacifier into her mouth, scowled, pulled it out, then stuck it in again.

Then she laid her head against Melonie's chest, subdued.

She walked back and forth, beneath the big spreading trees lining the driveway and around the ranch house, keeping the little one in the cool shade.

And when Jace came to get her a half hour later, she didn't want to let the baby go.

"I'm fine holding her," she whispered. Ava had finally dozed off against her shoulder. "I thought I'd sit in one of these porch rockers with her. If that's all right?"

"It's more than all right," he told her. He followed her up the steps, then drew the teakwood rocker farther from the wall. And when she settled into one, he took a seat in the other. "I'm sorry I ran out on you back at the house."

She arched one eyebrow in his direction.

"It wasn't my brightest move, I know. Five minutes wouldn't have made a difference, and the girls were in good hands. I'm not sure why I left like that."

"You did just become an instant daddy."

"And the county contacted me about filing for legal guardianship. When I told the social worker I'd like to adopt the girls, she said we either have to wait a long time for the courts to declare them abandoned, or get signed papers from Valencia that she's giving up her rights."

"Walking away and signing them away are two very different things." She patted the baby's back as she rocked.

"And no one knows where she is."

"Give Lizzie forty-eight hours and I expect she'd have an address for you. Probably less. She was an investigative reporter before she got pulled into a desk job at a ridiculously young age. She's got connections."

"But do we want to stir the pot?"

She understood the question. "Because she might want to come back and take over with the girls?"

Regret darkened his expression. "I'm not wishing their mother away. There's been enough heartache in this extended family to last a lifetime. But if she's in a bad frame of mind, would coming back help the girls? Or hurt them?"

"Will realizing their mother abandoned them help them or hurt in the future?"

He winced slightly. "That will be a hard thing to face, I expect."

"That's one of the things your grandmother protected you from," she noted softly. "By pushing for a solid home for you, she gave you a normal life. From the sounds of things, if Barbara had kept you, your life would have been quite different."

"You want me to play nice with her."

She shook her head slightly. "I'm talking about understanding. Maybe putting three decades under the microscope and seeing why people made the choices they did. This isn't about her mean-spiritedness or a racist attitude toward a grandson. It's easy to look back and find fault with decisions people made years ago." She dropped her eyes to the sleeping baby in her arms. "It's much more difficult to make those decisions right now."

He drew a breath. Then he folded his hands. "I hear you. And if you asked me a week ago, I'd have said I was a fair man, schooled to think things through. Figure things out. Then decide accordingly. So maybe I need to do some serious praying about what I want to have happen and what should happen. Because it's a really muddy pond from where I'm sitting."

The promised rain began to fall. A summer rain, waking up the quiet dust of the graveled barnyard with each initial drop.

"We wait for the storm to pass, the skies to brighten. It always clears eventually."

"You're right."

She didn't mind hearing that at all because she was pretty sure he might have a different opinion when she showed him some of her ideas for Hardaway Ranch.

"I'm going to go check on Annie. You sure you don't want me to tuck Ava into bed?"

She shook her head. "Nope, we're good right here. What if she wakes up crying when we lay her down, wakes up her sister and then we've got two fretful babies? Peace and quiet is always better."

"Can't argue that. Tea?"

"Yes, thanks." She smiled up at him. "Sweet tea, a front porch rocker and a sleepin' baby. I might just imagine myself down South after all."

Chapter Nine

The sight of Melonie, cradling Ava, not worried about her time or her work…and he knew she cared a lot about both those things.

Yet here she was, comforting a small child she barely knew.

A gust of wind swept in with the rain.

He took a lap blanket from the glider and laid it around Ava and Melonie. "Those gusts have a chill in them."

"Thank you, Jace."

He went inside.

Zeke was still sleeping on the small sofa. Lizzie sat nearby. Heath had gone off to the fields to check on the sheep with a couple of hands. Rain didn't bother sheep. A bad storm might send them into a huddle, but normal rain was no big deal.

Annie slept on upstairs.

He felt superfluous all of a sudden. And restless.

Cookie was out back, grilling ribs for dinner. Corrie was working in the vegetable garden they'd created. And here he was, with nothing to do when there was so very much to do.

"I suggest you take a minute to breathe." Lizzie came into the kitchen, grabbed a coffee pod and brewed herself a steaming mug.

"I'd have gotten that for you."

She shrugged. "Little guy is sound asleep, I need to get some wedding stuff done and the babies are both napping. I'm grabbing the minutes I can, same as Heath. I think this is how it's going to be," she warned him. "The minute you think you've got clear sailing, something goes wrong and a mad scramble ensues. Rosie said a few kids in town had a bug like this. It ran its course and was done in a couple of days."

"Shouldn't they see a doctor?"

"Corrie calls it the three-day rule," she told him. "If their fever doesn't come down with meds, call the doctor. If they get suddenly worse, call the doctor. Or if there's no change for the better by day three, call the doctor."

"So we wait?" Irritated, he scrubbed his hand along the nape of his neck. "I don't do waiting well."

She raised her coffee mug and clinked it against the glass of tea. "Welcome to parenthood. Maybe we can form a support group." She grinned, teasing. "Only new, uncertain parents need apply."

"Can I ask you something?"

"Sure."

"It's about your sister."

Lizzie lifted an eyebrow. "Don't ask me to divulge intense sister secrets, Jace. I value my life."

"The scar on her face. Backside of the left cheek. How'd she get that?"

"Not my story to tell. And not a topic she brings up. So good luck. But tread lightly. And most folks don't notice it now because of the way she wears her hair." She studied him. "But you did."

He was not about to mention dancing in the grass with Melonie. Dipping her. Then seeing the long curve of the scar just inside her hairline. "When we were working."

"Mmm-hmm." She sipped her coffee. Gazed at him. Then she smiled. "Work'll do it, Jace. Every time."

He flushed.

She wouldn't know it because the tint of his skin hid it, but the minute he did, Lizzie grinned.

Melonie had said she used to be an investigative reporter. He realized he wasn't getting much by the oldest Fitzgerald sister. "Melonie said that if I wanted to find Valencia, you might be able to help."

"Oh." Doubt changed her expression. "Are you sure you want to stir that up?"

"Not at all. But I need to have legal recourse with the girls. Gilda has already spoken with the county."

"A precipitous move on her part."

"Tell me about it. But we need to have things in place in case Valencia comes back. Except how do we keep a mother from her children?" He folded his arms, conflicted. "That seems so wrong."

"Speaking as the daughter of a runaway father, I can heartily say that it's never a black-and-white situation, Jace. But if we're looking after the safety of the children, then we have to look at any possible dangers to them. What if Valencia takes them and leaves them alone in some other place? Where there's no sweet uncle ready to open his doors and his heart? She's gone off and used false names before."

Gilda had said as much.

"Can we risk that?" she continued. "I can do a search," she went on as she moved back toward the living room. "I've got connections and it's pretty hard to hide these days. But you have to make sure it's what you really, truly want."

He didn't want it. He didn't know this sister, didn't know her story, her choices. Why would she take off now? Did something make her flee? Or did she simply abandon her babies? "I'll think about it." He'd set down Melonie's tea. He lifted it again. "Pray on it, too. I don't know what's right or wrong in all this."

Lizzie's face echoed that statement.

"But I know I want and need to do the right thing. Whatever that is."

He took Melonie's tea to the porch.

She'd dozed off with that sweet baby in her arms. Ava was nestled against Melonie's shoulder, and the pair of them sent a surge of protectiveness through him.

He set the tea down and put a firm check on his emotions.

He *should* want to protect these baby girls, his nieces.

He couldn't feel the same way about Melonie. They'd work together, help Gilda with her house. Then winter would sweep in and he'd spend the long, cold months running sheep. Counting lambs. Winter lambing was always much more labor intensive. The Middletons had run cattle. Not a huge operation, but a profitable one. They made do. But that had all ended when he was a boy. His father had dreamed of starting again. They'd envisioned running Angus together on the broad sweep of land that used to be Middleton property.

But then Sean Fitzgerald bought the land from his grandfather for a fair price. Once property values began to skyrocket the last decade, his father stopped talking about beginning again.

Then he was gone. They had the small stretch of land behind the house. Big enough to house the horses. Maybe a pig or two to put in the freezer. Not enough to stake a beginning. And with contracting jobs few and far between…

He'd finish this job. Do his best to make Gilda happy and bring Melonie's vision to life.

Then he'd go to Sun Valley next spring. As originally planned.

And Melonie would go back to her quest for success.

She shifted slightly. The small blanket slipped down.

He lifted it and gently settled it back where it had been.

He couldn't see the scar now. That side of her pretty face was obscured.

But having seen it made him wonder about her. The woman behind the classy clothes and strong work ethic. Seeing her in the dirt today, seeing that scar, he realized there was more to this woman than he first thought.

But she was cradling the very reason he couldn't explore that. His parents had always put their kids first.

He wouldn't be the man they raised him to be if he did any less.

"Now, that is a pleasant sight," Perched on the front porch railing, Melonie lifted her coffee mug in salute as Corrie walked the double stroller down the driveway toward Rosie's place three days later. "Two happy babies and one busy five-year-old, fully recovered."

Jace was standing just inside the screen door. He lifted his coffee in Corrie's direction, too, and agreed. "I'm glad they're better."

"Me, too. And we can be thankful for Corrie and Rosie, because now we can return to work."

She was glad when he kept their conversation work-related. "The supplies for my place are being delivered this morning. I'm heading over there to accept delivery, then I'm backtracking to Hardaway Ranch to check on the roofers. They're supposed to start today if the Dumpsters have been dropped off and…" He lifted his phone when it buzzed. "That's my cue that they've arrived and tear-off will commence within the hour. Listen, Melonie." He came through the door with a to-go cup in one hand and his phone in the other. "Why don't you work here where it's quiet?"

She slid her gaze from the busy sheep barn to the horse stables, then to the ranch house, where three hearty stockmen were having a quick bite of sausage, bacon, home fries, eggs, Texas toast and pancakes.

Then she brought her gaze back to his. "Your idea of quiet and mine are on opposite ends of the spectrum," she told him. "Gilda's due here anytime," she reminded him. "And while I'm sympathetic to her cause, I can't imagine getting a whole lot done if she's looking over my shoulder." She hesitated, then faced him directly. "Do you mind me working there?" she asked outright. "I figured on letting the morning sun dry up some of the rain so I'll work in your office at first, if that's all right." She lifted her laptop bag. "Then garden duty this afternoon."

"Shouldn't we hire someone to finish the rest of the garden?" he asked as he moved down the stairs.

"Except I enjoy it." He stopped when she said that. He didn't look back, but he paused, unmoving. "I like working in the dirt. Making things pretty. And seeing them stay pretty for years to come."

He hesitated for another moment, then continued down the stairs. "All right."

He drove off in his truck.

He didn't invite her to ride along.

That was okay. She'd need her own transportation later that day, but a part of her wished he'd offered her a ride.

He didn't, and when she got to the house a half hour later, the supplies were neatly stacked in the garage and his truck was gone. Off to Gilda's, she supposed.

He'd left the door unlocked. She moved through the newly opened living area, then past what remained of the bathroom.

When she heard him return less than an hour later, he didn't seek her out to say hi. Or check on progress.

The sound of his saw cut the morning quiet, followed by the pneumatic snap of a precise air hammer.

She stayed in his simple office space, the door shut, until she heard him call her name just before lunch.

She hit Save, got up and opened the door. Jace wasn't on the far side of the room like she expected.

He was there. Right there. And a trail of bright red blood marked the path behind him.

There was no time to think. Or swoon, which would have been her first choice.

She grabbed a towel from the adjacent linen closet. "How bad?"

"Nothing some salve and duct tape won't cure. But I can't do it one-handed."

Salve? Duct tape? "Please tell me you're kidding."

He looked positively perplexed.

"Anything that's bleeding that badly needs professional help, Jace."

"Or salve and duct tape. Seriously, if I could do it myself, I would, but I can't. Even if I tear the tape with my teeth."

She looked behind him, and sure enough, there were scraps of tape on the floor where the dolt had tried to treat himself. "I'll drive you to the ER."

His eyebrows arched. "All that time and money lost? Listen, my father used to say that if it bleeds well, bandage it. We'll know soon enough if it's not right."

She was not about to argue with his late father's advice. She motioned forward. "Kitchen."

He moved that way.

"Keep the pressure on."

"Got it."

Her stomach had risen right up into her throat at the sight of that blood, a leftover reaction from her childhood trauma. Since then she'd steered clear of anything blood-related, including rare meat.

She swallowed hard to gather her strength, turned the water on to a warm temperature and lifted the bottle of antibacterial soap. "Put your arm under here."

He did, letting the warm water sluice over the wound.

"Was this from your saw?" she asked as she finished scrubbing her hands.

"A piece of wood that bounced back."

"Equally unhygienic."

"Actually, it looked pretty good until I messed it up by bleeding on it."

"Jace." She didn't want to do this. She wasn't sure she *could* do this. But she also realized he might be right, that it wasn't necessarily an emergency-room injury. "I'll try not to hurt you."

"If you could see the scrub-brush techniques ER nurses use, you would not say those words. They're earnest," he told her, eyes wide on purpose.

He made her laugh.

She was laughing at his expression while cleaning a life-threatening wound. Well, maybe not life-threatening, she decided as she continued to flush the area. But not exactly minor, either.

"Are you sure you don't need stitches?"

"This only needs some Steri-Strips and a gauze pad under the duct tape to keep the duct tape from sticking to the gash. The first-aid box is right up there." He motioned to a shelf by the back door, and when she eyed the dust on it, he had the nerve to grin.

"That's why the case closes real tight," he told her. "To keep everything inside nice and clean."

Oh, brother.

"Those butterfly-shaped things. They're made to pull the sides of the cut together."

The last thing she wanted to think about was pulling sides together.

"Then maybe two of those gauze pads," he continued. "There's a fresh roll of duct tape right there alongside."

Yup. A thick roll of silvery gray industrial tape held a place of honor. "No medical tape? That nice, clean white stuff?"

"Doesn't stick," he answered. "Duct tape is made to stick. Gets me right back to work."

Inside the first-aid kit was a selection of bandages and pads, antibiotic salve and the duct tape right next to a clean bag containing tweezers, a needle and a tiny scalpel-like instrument that she refused to contemplate. "You have a personal ER right here," she muttered. "What are the super sharp scissors for?"

"Fish hooks," he told her. "They snap right

through them, the normal-sized ones that is. We use them as needed."

Have mercy. She left his arm under the running water while she set things out and cut two lengths of tape. "If you get infected…"

"I'll go right over to the little clinic in Council and they'll put me on antibiotics. This isn't my first rodeo, Miss Mellie."

He said her name sweetly. It was funny, but kind, too, as if maybe he realized that binding wounds wasn't exactly her cup of tea. Of course, the expression of fear on her face might have given him a clue.

She pressed a clean towel to the area surrounding the wound, then applied the salve. Generously.

"Well, not much can hope to live through that," he told her. He grinned encouragement and approval. "Now the Steri-Strips. And then the pads."

"Thank you, doctor."

He cringed. "Sorry."

She applied the butterfly bandages, then followed with the pads and strips of tape. "These are going to hurt when you pull them off," she warned. "Duct tape is not meant to be used on arm hair."

He flexed his arm, then nodded. "It'll only

hurt for a minute. And look." He moved his arm back and forth. "Full mobility. You did great."

"Only because I didn't faint," she muttered as she cleaned up the area. "Are you at least going to rest a little? Give it a chance to bind?"

"And not work?" He stared at her in disbelief. "Then what would be the point of this? I want to be able to jump on Gilda's job when the roofing's complete, so there's no time to waste. And I can't bring the girls here until I've got this place done." He glanced around the house before he brought his attention back to her. "They need to come home, don't they?"

Sweet words from the man facing her. The kind of man who did what was needed, when needed.

She thought men like this only existed in stories. "You're right."

"If I need a hand putting things in place, are you available? I've got those last two-by-sixes ready to install."

"Yes, if only to keep you from killing yourself."

He sent her a lazy grin. "There's a comforting thought. But nice to know you can come through in the clutch, ma'am."

"Just don't sue me when you're fighting a major-league infection next week."

"On my honor. Grab hold of this here." They

set the last two parts of the half wall together. She marveled at the precise moves of his hands, even with an injured forearm. He triggered the gun with his right hand as if it was nothing to do it one-handed.

She'd used air hammers before. They had a solid kick and buck.

Not in his hands. He nailed the supports like a skilled craftsman, and when they finished with the framing lumber, she helped him with the wallboard. "Do you need me for the wainscoting?" she asked when the plasterboard was in place.

"No, I'm using the little gun. But thank you. This keeps me on schedule." Turning, he gave her an easy shoulder nudge. When she slanted her attention up, he nodded to the nearly renovated space. "I couldn't have gotten this far without you. Thank you, Melonie." Holding her gaze, he smiled.

She could get lost in those eyes, all velvety brown. Warm. Happy. Inviting.

This was an invitation she needed to turn down. "Simple teamwork, Jace. To get to project number two we must complete project number one."

His eyes lost the humor. He took a breath as if contemplating her words, then nodded. "That's the plan."

She went outside.

She'd squelched that light in his eyes on purpose, when it was about the last thing she wanted to do.

Are you that in love with the idea of your own show? Your chance to shine in the sun?

She wasn't, no. It wasn't about the show or the magazine or making a big deal of herself.

She stuck the small shovel into the ground pretty fiercely because it wasn't about her. She knew who she was. But in the back of her mind, lingering still, was the memory of the look of disappointment she saw in her father's face while she was lying in that hospital bed.

She'd failed him. She'd failed the horse, she'd failed the famed Fitzgerald name, she'd failed, pure and simple. Now she wanted to feel successful on her own terms. To show Tim Fitzgerald that even though she couldn't sit saddle like her sisters, she wasn't a failure.

Would he even know? her conscience argued. *Or care?*

Probably not. She knew that. But she'd carry the satisfaction with her. That would be enough.

She made a quick trip to the garden nursery in Council, and when she had two hanging baskets, three Knock Out rosebushes, wave petunias, wax begonias and eight different baby mum plants tucked into the car, she drove back to Jace's home.

He was gone.

She'd pre-dug the holes for the roses, and the begonias were an easy task. A stack of bagged black mulch stood at the driveway's edge.

It was quiet. Too quiet. It had been fun doing this with Jace a few days before. She took out her phone, hit a music app and when it started playing new country, she chose an oldies mix and started again.

Better, she decided when the strains of Glenn Miller's orchestra filled the yard.

She'd danced to "Moonlight Serenade" as a teen. And she'd boogied her way across the stage to "Pennsylvania 6-5000" a year later.

Corrie and her sisters had cheered her on. Corrie never made her feel like dancing wasn't as cool as show-riding. Neither had the girls. But her father, the man who sent roses to Charlotte and Lizzie when they brought home silver cups of victory, never once came to a recital. Never once brought or sent a bouquet. Corrie tried to cover for him after one performance. The roses had come, and she'd pretended she didn't know that Corrie had phoned the order in.

But when she thanked her father the next morning, his look of surprise gave it away.

"For I know the plans I have for you," says

the Lord. "They are plans for good and not for disaster, to give you a future and a hope."

The uplifting verse from Jeremiah helped. That and a few other favorite scriptures, words of encouragement that helped show a true father's love. God's love.

By the time the new roses were set and watered, the trees offered sweet shade from the warm sun. She planted the smaller flowers quickly, and when she was done, she smiled.

She was just lifting her first bulky bag of mulch when Jace pulled in. He climbed out of the truck, tipped back his cowboy hat, lifted the heavy bag of mulch from her hands and whistled lightly. "You've done it."

"Do you like it?"

"Love it," he admitted. "My mom would have loved it, too. I don't know if she ever thought of black fabric to block weeds. And it works?"

"Like a charm. Between that and the mulch, keeping these gardens up should be a breeze."

He shouldered the mulch and strode across the sidewalk looking way too good for her not to notice. "Here?" He turned when he neared the porch and caught her look of appreciation.

He grinned.

She ignored him, and nodded. "Yes, thanks." *Play it cool. Maintain your distance.* "If you set it down, I'll open it and spread it."

"I'll dump them carefully, then you can maneuver it," he argued. "There is no reason for you to be lifting big, heavy bags like this."

She looked everywhere but at him. "Thank you."

"You're welcome. Got some sun today, eh?"

Setting one dusty hand to her cheek was a giveaway. She'd thought it was the rising warmth heating her cheeks. Nope. "I forgot to put on sunscreen. Duh."

He winced. "I don't have any here. I'm not exactly the burn-and-freckle type."

Oh, he wasn't. He was absolutely the to-die-for tawny-skin type. "I know. You've got gorgeous skin."

Did she really just say that? Out loud?

She'd bent over to pat down the fabric around the second rosebush and if she could stay there forever, eyes down, she would.

Since that was impossible, she stood and dusted her hands against the sides of her old capris.

"Gorgeous, huh?"

Now it wasn't just the sun's rays heating her cheeks.

He stepped closer. And then he tucked one finger under her chin and lifted it gently. His voice went husky as he studied her face. Studied her. "I think you've got this confused, Melonie."

She raised her eyes to his. He gazed back at her with such a look of wonder that she was pretty sure her heart melted on the spot.

"You're the gorgeous one here." His hand touched her neck as if it was meant to be there. His voice, already deep, went deeper, and if her heart hadn't already gone soft, it did right then.

His gaze dropped from her eyes to her lips, then he touched his mouth to hers.

He smelled of sawdust and timber and fresh air, and when he deepened the kiss, she stretched up on tiptoe to ease the height difference between them.

"Melonie." He said her name like a summer night's whisper.

"I know." He'd pulled her in for a hug, a hug that felt like she was where she belonged. Of course, she wasn't. "We shouldn't be doing this."

"Whereas I was thinking we should be doing it on a regular basis," he teased. The scruff of his beard brushed her sunburned cheek, and when she winced, he drew back. "Ouch, sorry. I'll be sure to shave." He put his hand against her cheek—the scarred cheek—then met her gaze again. "I don't want to ever do anything that hurts you, Melonie."

She reached up her hand to cover his. "Then we need to wake up because this can't end well. We both know it."

He stepped back as if in full agreement. "You are absolutely right. We need to stop this. Right now."

That was about the last thing she wanted him to say, but it was the sensible thing, so she nodded. Even though she didn't really want to.

"We'll take it up again when we finish the gardens."

That wasn't what she meant, but he knew that. She went back to spreading the mulch while old-time music played in the background. Jace went through ten bags of mulch, then threw the empties into the construction dump. "I'm going to start on the bathroom."

"Wonderful." She didn't look up. "When we…" She stopped herself purposely. "When *you* get the girls to bed tonight, if all goes well, can I have you look at a few possible ideas for Gilda's place?"

"Absolutely. Meet you on the porch?"

He was teasing her.

She threw him a semi-scathing look. "In the well-lit living room with chaperones, mister. I get that we're attracted to each other."

He tipped back the brim of his black hat and didn't grin. He just lifted an eyebrow slightly. And quirked his jaw.

"But we're like two trains, heading in opposite directions."

"Up here, in the Wild West, we know that a train might go in one direction…but it always comes back," he reminded her as he headed for the door. "Because it's a train, darlin'. And the track runs both ways. I don't see one sign saying beautiful women can't fix houses in Idaho. Not one anti-house statute that I know of."

He had to be kidding.

One look at his face said he wasn't. But when he read her doubtful expression, the smile left his face. "Not as big and grand, I expect."

What could she say? Gilda's job was the exception, not the norm. The area wasn't thriving. It was barely existing. A few rich ranches and a slate of empty houses and run-down farms. "Jace—"

"Gotta get back to it."

She'd hurt his feelings. She longed to go after him and apologize, but she'd pointed out a significant chasm. She wasn't ashamed of wanting to do well. It didn't define her. She wasn't foolish enough or pretentious enough to let that happen.

But doing a good job and having a career mattered to her and she refused to have to justify her choices anymore. Ever. She'd been given the magazine job because of who her father was. It wasn't like she was a well-known designer who'd earned her way up the ladder at twenty-eight years old. Nepotism had secured her job, then she'd had the guts and grit to prove she could do it.

Her father hadn't made her do that, and she knew why. He doubted her strength. Her capabilities. Her ambition.

Why do you need to prove anything to him? He's a cheat and a scoundrel. Why does this matter?

She spread mulch and realized it might take a team of therapists to reason that one out. She didn't owe her father anything. But just once in her life, just once, she'd like to think she'd done something to make him proud. He was the only biological parent she had…

And it shouldn't be too much to ask him to care.

She understood the reality, but the kid inside—the little girl she once was—was still waiting for that bunch of roses. A bouquet that he actually ordered and paid for. A bouquet that would never, ever come.

Chapter Ten

Not good enough.

Not rich enough.

Not opportunistic enough.

His hard-hit town, the town his family helped build, wasn't wealthy enough for Melonie.

You knew this. You knew it from the moment you set eyes on her, when she dismissed you with a single shrug of those pretty shoulders. You knew it and still you kissed her.

He knew better for a number of reasons, which meant applying the brakes one hundred percent.

He didn't want to. That kiss—that amazingly beautiful, wonderful kiss—had set his head to thinking and his pulse to jumping, but it wasn't just the kiss. It was seeing her with Ava, cuddled in that rocker. Seeing her pretend to nibble Ava's baby toes, and play peek-a-boo and laugh at the little blue-eyed blonde that seemed to think Melonie was pretty special.

What if the toddler got too attached? Would that mess her up when Melonie left next year?

He leveled the concrete and set the new tub about the same time the electrician showed up to lay in additional wiring. He turned the bathroom over to him, and walked out back.

Bubba plodded his way. The old horse almost smiled, happy to see him. He wasn't used to Jace being gone so much, and in his advanced years, the gelding liked routine. He bobbed his head and when Jace laid out apple slices, Bubba accepted them greedily. And when Jace reached out to stroke his neck, the trusty mount leaned in like a faithful dog.

"I'm done out front."

He and the horse both turned toward Melonie's voice as Bonnie came their way from the opposite direction.

"I'm going to head back to Pine Ridge."

He nodded.

She indicated the horses with a look. "What will you do with them if you decide to move next spring?"

"Leave them."

She didn't look at him. Just them. His two old, loyal friends.

"I don't have the money to buy acreage in Sun

Valley. It's much more upscale than this." He swept the broad, beautiful valley a long look. "But there's work there, so it's a trade-off."

She brushed her hands against her thighs. "Life's full of those, I suppose."

"How many trade-offs have you had to make, Melonie?"

He didn't mean to sound harsh, but he did and she jerked slightly. Then she leveled a cool look his way, and shrugged one shoulder. "Practically none." She walked away as Bonnie sidled up to the fence, looking for a handout.

He sliced another apple. They were from last year's crop and wilted now.

The horses didn't care.

They thought the less-than-perfect treats were wonderful.

Melonie's engine started as Bonnie lapped at his hand, happy with such a small thing. How he wished the woman walking away felt the same way.

By the time he got to the ranch, Corrie had walked the girls back up to the big house. As he climbed the porch steps, shrieks of joy and giggles came through the wooden screen door. Ava and Annie were in the living room. Baby toys were scattered across the floor.

Melonie wasn't inside. She wasn't on the

porch, and although he didn't want to listen for her voice, he did.

Nothing.

"Hey, Papa Jace!" Lizzie had snagged a handful of cookies from the cookie jar. She handed him two. "Cookie said supper's an hour off because he had a slight kitchen emergency…"

"Emergency?" Jace had been working here for over a dozen years. Cookie had never so much as had a misstep, much less an emergency. "Is he all right?"

"Fine. But the first pot of stew might have cooked dry while he was up the drive, visiting the girls."

Cookie didn't go up the drive. He didn't lose focus. Ever. "He went up to Rosie's?"

"Thought he'd turned the pot down to simmer. Must have forgotten. He took cookies over to Corrie and Rosie."

To Corrie and Rosie…

Ah.

Jace raised his eyebrows. "So maybe it wasn't the babies snagging his attention," he mused softly.

"Miss Corrie Satterly may have found herself a beau!" Lizzie whispered, making sure no one was around to hear it. "You make sure to keep this to yourself, all right?"

"No one will hear it from me," he promised.

He pretended not to notice that Melonie was heading their way from the direction of the horse stables. She had her computer bag with her. He averted his eyes intentionally, then got down on the floor to play with the girls. But when she didn't come in, he had to wonder where she'd gotten off to.

Then he heard Gilda's voice.

"So Gilda hung out here today?" he asked Lizzie from his spot on the floor.

"First she went to old Mr. Palmenteer's to take him some of Sally Ann's jam. They had a conversation worth having, according to Gilda. Then on to the Carrington Ranch to tell Sally how much folks loved her jams and jellies."

"The recluse is making the rounds," he mused.

Lizzie rolled a ball to Ava. Ava eyed the ball, then Lizzie, before deciding she didn't want to throw it back while sitting down. She crawled to the couch, grabbed hold and stood up. But then the ball was halfway across the room. She studied the ball, then the adults, trying to solve the problem.

"Then she came here with two more jars of jam and surprised us all by going up the drive, on her own, to visit the kids. And Zeke said she even sat down in the grass with the girls."

He didn't want to feel compassion for the old woman. She'd made her choices. Years of them.

Decades. So now she was trying to ingratiate herself to her neighbors and estranged family. Buying her ticket to heaven, he supposed. Except it didn't work that way, and he was pretty sure Gilda Hardaway knew that.

He couldn't hear Melonie's voice over the babies' babbles, but he heard Gilda's approving exclamations, which meant Melonie was showing her ideas.

He didn't want to intervene, or rain on their parade, but fancy designs didn't always work. Load-bearing walls and structural integrity were two things that some folks were willing to sacrifice in favor of a particular look. Too much sacrifice meant the roof might come down on your head.

He jutted his chin toward the porch. "Do you mind keeping an eye on these two while I butt into that porch discussion?"

"Not in the slightest."

Jace got up from the floor and headed to the porch, where Melonie and his grandmother sat. "Ladies."

Gilda looked up quickly when he came through the door. Her smile was more like a wince, but she aimed it straight at him. "I'm glad you're here, Jason. Melonie was just sharing some ideas with me and we wanted you in on the conversation."

"To see what's doable and what might need tweaking," said Melonie.

"I might have been able to save you both some time if I'd previewed the ideas." He made the comment lightly, but when Melonie lifted slow, gray eyes to his, he knew she caught the shielded reprimand.

"We're open to adjustments as needed," she said with candor, then poked Gilda's arm lightly. "But your grandmother knows this house far better than we do, so I thought I'd run some thoughts by her first."

"And I want it different." Insistence sharpened Gilda's response. "It never had the right feel the first go-around, so this one needs to be better. Done right," she insisted. "From top to bottom. And maybe not so walled-in here and there."

"We can open the first floor some, sure." Jace went around behind the ladies while Melonie brought up a new page. He pointed to the wall separating the kitchen from what must have been a grand living room at one time. "With a support beam here." He pointed to the current wall separating the two rooms. "And widening this here, we can keep the integrity of the structure and open things up."

"It's harder to keep secrets in a more open house." Gilda's voice softened.

Hairs stood up along Jace's neck.

He didn't want to hear about her secrets. He didn't care. The past and its pack of lies needed to be left there.

Just then, one of the babies shrieked in glee.

He started back for the door.

"You don't need to see any more?" Gilda asked. "No more advice?"

"At the moment there are two more important things to tend to," he told her. "This is my time with the girls. I was under the impression that consultation over the design layout of your house was going to take place later. Once they were in bed."

Gilda's mouth drew down.

Not in anger. But in sorrow. Because he sounded like a pretentious jerk after being a guardian for a matter of days.

"You go on, of course." She waved him off, apologetic. "I should be heading out now, anyway."

"I thought you said the roofers were working late." Melonie had the decency to look concerned while he acted like a dolt.

"A little noise and kabobble never hurt anyone." Gilda started to stand. Her dress snagged on the glider's edge. She began to tip slightly.

"Whoa." Jace grabbed hold of her arm quickly so she wouldn't fall.

"I'm fine."

"Of course you are." Melonie tucked the laptop aside and stood. "And you're not going anywhere except right here for supper and time with your great-granddaughters. They need that family time, it's the best thing for them. To have their Gee-Gee there—"

When Gilda looked blank, Melonie took Gilda's other arm and said, "Great-Grandma."

"I've never heard such a thing." Gilda frowned while Jace made sure they'd unsnagged the simple cotton dress she'd worn from the glider. "But I might like it."

"Down South there is a plethora of names for grandparents," Melonie told her as they moved toward the door. She must have showered since she'd returned because the scent of strawberries and something else—coconut, maybe—filled the air when she moved. "Meemaw, Mawmaw, Gammie, Mimi, Lovie, Neenee."

Gilda seemed shocked. "Not a soul your way just says Grandma?"

"Not too many, although my maternal grandmother was Nana. She and my father didn't get along and he made it very difficult for her to have any time with us."

"I am so sorry, my dear."

Jace opened the screened door as Gilda paused.

"Those family divisions are so wrong," she

muttered, as if scolding herself. Then she took a breath and sighed. "I only wish I'd known that as a younger woman."

Yup. A late harvester, just like they talked about in the Bible. How God paid all in equal amounts, even if they came late to the table of believers. As a working man, Jace understood the injustice in that. As a Christian, he understood the generosity God offered. Resolving the two...well, that was the problem, wasn't it?

The babies babbled when they moved into the living room. Ava had left the couch, and when she spotted Melonie she ducked her head and crawled as fast as those stocky little arms and legs allowed. Then she grabbed hold of Melonie's legs, and pulled herself up. "Bah!" she implored, then raised her hands up. Straight up, standing on her own. "Bah, bah!"

Melonie took a small step back. Then another, creating a span between her and the baby. Then she stooped low while the rest watched. "You want me, sweetie? Come get me."

Ava stared at her, then Jace and Gilda, as if questioning Melonie's right to move away.

Then she brought that blue-eyed gaze right back to Melonie. She stuck her two little arms out and waved them. "Bah! Bah! Bah!"

Melonie nodded, smiling, arms out. "I'm right here." She spoke in a voice laced with sweet encouragement and joy. "Come on, Ava. You can do this."

The baby squawked one more time, but seemed to size up the situation despite her vocal protest and then—with all of them watching, scarcely daring to breathe—she took a step.

Her expression changed.

She seemed a little bit frightened and very excited all at once. She stood in place, bobbed up and down, almost dancing, then took a second step toward Melonie.

Oh, her smile!

A baby grin, from ear to ear as she chortled about her success before taking that final step, the one that brought her back to Melonie's very pretty legs. "Bah!" She screeched the word, laughing. "Bah!"

"You did it!" Melonie scooped her up, blew raspberry kisses along Ava's pudgy little neck and laughed with her. "You walked, schnookums! Good job!" She handed her right over to Jace. "Papa Jace is so proud of you, too."

His heart, which had gone sour earlier that day, unsoured right quick when Melonie handed him that baby so that he could share in the joy of those first steps. Sure, she'd gone to Melonie. Ava had developed a sweet spot for Melonie from day one. And it would have been so easy and natural to hog the moment.

She didn't.

He'd pretty much intimated that she grew up as a spoiled rich girl, yet who was it working on her knees in the dark Idaho soil earlier that afternoon?

Melonie.

And who handed over the beautiful child into his arms to share a milestone moment?

Melonie.

"They'll need baths today." Lizzie stood as Annie crawled toward Jace to see what all the excitement was about. "They had some fun outside earlier and since supper's going to be later than normal, should we bathe them now?"

"It makes sense," Gilda said. "I'm not as mobile as I used to be, but I can warm towels. I used to warm towels for your baths," she told Jace, as if there weren't thirty empty years yawning in between. "You were born just shy of Christmas and it was a long, cold winter. We had such good heat that I'd warm the towels while Barbara bathed you. Then I'd wrap that towel around you and you'd snuggle in, just so."

He wasn't sure what to say because he wanted to throw a million questions at her.

He couldn't. Not now. Maybe not ever. But the image of this old woman, as she might have been three decades back, wrapping him up in a warm towel and then snuggling him dry… He had to choke back emotion from his voice. "We can use the downstairs bathroom. I'll run the water."

He escaped into the bathroom long enough to recover his wits.

When she'd told him that the Middletons adopted him at a year old, he hadn't given much thought to the year prior. Only the years after.

Now she'd painted more of the picture. His father gone. And she and his mother, caring for him. Nurturing him.

It didn't compute.

How did you give away something you loved?

He started back to the living room and saw Gilda making funny faces at Ava. Yes, he could almost see her doing that with him, a long time ago.

Almost—but not quite.

"The mark's gone." Melonie swallowed hard as they finished bathing and diapering the babies about forty minutes later.

"The what?"

She looked from Jace to Lizzie and Gilda, then back. "The mark," she whispered. "To tell them apart."

"You marked them again?" Lizzie's voice was a mix of surprise and admiration. "I thought you were amazing because you could always tell them apart so I just followed along."

"Jace?"

He put up his hands. "No clue. Unless they're sleeping and we do the hand thing that Rosie suggested."

"There's got to be a way." Melonie stared at the girls.

"How about Corrie? Or Rosie?"

Corrie came into the room at that moment. "Sweet, clean babies! Just in time to have some mush, little darlings. Oh, you smell so good!" She got down and smooched both girls, then realized the four adults were watching her. "What's wrong?"

"Who are you kissing?"

Corrie's brow knitted. "Excuse me?"

"I mean the babies," Jace explained. "Which baby were you just kissing?"

Corrie looked from him, to the other adults, and then the twins. "You've gone and mixed up these sweet babies, and isn't that a bit of a pickle?" She stared up at their woebegone faces and burst out laughing. "You know twenty years ago this would be more difficult, but there is information at your fingertips every which way nowadays," she reminded them. "How were you telling them apart before?"

A sheepish expression darkened Jace's demeanor. "The colors. The pink and purple. I changed one at a time, so it wasn't a problem."

"Well, there are worse things in the world than being called the wrong name for a spell, but there must be a way to distinguish them. Some little identifier," she reasoned.

"I'd marked them."

Corrie tipped her gaze to Melonie. "Say what, child?"

"With what was supposed to be a permanent marker," grumbled Melonie. "I've examined both feet. No dot," she explained as Heath and Zeke came through the back door. Heath kicked off his boots and the little guy followed suit.

"So now they're not dressed and there's no distinguishing mark because neither one has a birthmark or mole to help us out."

"Or a strawberry mark like you had," Gilda said to Jace. "Right at the back of your neck, where the hairline is. It went away in time, most do, but neither one of these little beauties has a mark."

They shared troubled looks while the babies giggled, free from the constraints of clothing while the adults tried to figure out what to do.

"I can always tell them apart," bragged Zeke once he'd lined his boots up alongside his father's. "It's easy, once you know the secret."

The hopeful look on Jace's face was almost amusing, but Melonie didn't dare laugh...at least not yet. "You can tell them apart?"

"Easy-peasy," said the boy, then he turned toward the babies. "Annie. Ava!" He didn't speak loud, he kept his voice calm and low, with just a hint of excitement.

One baby turned.

Zeke fist-punched the air. "That's Ava. I know because Ava always turns when I do that. Annie doesn't."

Annie doesn't.

He dashed off to the front room while the adults faced one another. "What does that mean?" Jace asked. "Does Ava turn because she's trying to hear what's going on? Or does Annie not turn because she doesn't hear what's going on?" He lifted Ava while Corrie picked up Annie. "Could one of them be deaf?" he asked, and the sorrow in his voice highlighted the depth of emotion for two babies he'd only met a week before.

"They can do hearing tests, Jace."

"On babies?"

Heath nodded as he reached out a hand to Ava's still damp wisps of hair. "Then we'll know."

Jace hugged Ava to his chest until she squawked to get free. He took her out to the big front room, and when she wriggled to get down, he set her on the floor with a tender touch.

Then he watched as Corrie slipped a pink-and-yellow paisley romper onto Annie while Melonie did the same with a lilac version for Ava.

The supper bell clanged.

Heath and Lizzie slipped away with Zeke. Corrie lifted Annie. "I've got their supper ready and waiting and I expect that bath invigorated them."

"May I feed one of them?" Gilda hadn't said a word, but her face registered concern. "I'm not strong enough to carry one into the kitchen, but I can still lift a spoon and wipe a pretty little face."

"Of course you can," Melonie told her. "You're their great-grandma."

Jace stayed quiet, and when Melonie came back from the kitchen, he'd moved to the porch. She hung at the door for long, drawn seconds before she pushed it open.

He was standing at the rail, hands braced, chin down. She wanted to go to him. Tell him it would be all right, but would it?

She approached the rail, turned to lean her back against it, then stood beside him, silent. Praying.

"I didn't notice," he said finally. "I've been with these babies for over a week, and it took a five-year-old to point out the obvious. That one of the girls doesn't react to her name. Or overreacts to it, straining to hear. What kind of a person am I? What kind of dad will I be to them?" he went on, gruffly. "If I don't notice a big thing like that, how can I pretend to be the right person to do this? I don't know anything about babies. About raising kids. What kind of person has to go online and order three books about parenting because he doesn't have a clue how to do the right thing or even know what the right thing is?"

She stayed quiet as the sun set lower in the Western sky. Filtered through feathered bands of cirrus clouds, the oblique rays splayed coral and orange through the green-leafed trees, like an inspirational painting. And when he finally turned her way, she asked one simple question. "Do you love them?"

He didn't hesitate at all. "Absolutely. It would be impossible not to love them. They're adorable."

"Then you do exactly what your parents did with you at the very same age," she whispered.

That got his attention. He swallowed hard as reality set in.

"You love them. You stumble along, learning as you go like all new parents do, but as long as you're bound by that love, you'll do just fine, Jace. And if one of the girls has a hearing problem, then who better to be her champion than a big, rugged cowboy who knows how to wrestle cattle, birth lambs and wrangle a whole mess of hay under cover when rain threatens the outcome? If I were that little girl, either of them." She aimed a pointed look inside. "I'd pick you every time. And those two girls will grow up knowing they're blessed to have you on their side. And that's the truth of it, Jace. Even though you do have a grumpy side from time to time." She couldn't resist adding that last bit, mostly because it was true on occasion.

He still gazed out. But then he slanted his gaze her way. "I'm not grumpy."

She made a face, doubtful. "Of course not, my bad." When he growled lightly, she smiled. "It's not that you haven't had a few things to grumble about. It's that there's so much more to be grateful for, Jace. Your health. Your sister. Your faith, your home, even those two old horses you love so well." She folded her arms as the temperature dipped lower. "And this brand-new family you didn't know you had. I'd say your cup is overflowing." She crossed to the glider and lifted her laptop. "Go enjoy your time with the girls. I'm going to make some adjustments to my plan. We can go over them tomorrow. All right?"

She didn't really give him a choice because she moved toward the westward-facing porch stairs as she spoke.

"Melonie."

She turned at the top of the stairs.

He sighed and kept it simple, cowboy-style. "Thank you."

She dipped her chin slightly. Then she raised one finger and pretended to touch the brim of a nonexistent cowboy hat. "'Til tomorrow."

Chapter Eleven

Jace left a message for the pediatrician's office, then drove to the Hardaway Ranch to check on the roofing progress.

"Jace." The foreman moved his way and pointed out how far they'd come. "We're getting there."

"I'll say." The uppermost roof was done and the side wing was being retooled by a crew of four. "It's amazing how a good roof finishes the look of a place, isn't it?"

"In this case, it couldn't hurt," the foreman told him. "I've got two guys who can help you with demolition inside if you want. I can spare them for two days once this job is done. That would save them from a lull no one wants or can afford."

"Are they solid workers?"

"Wouldn't offer them if they weren't. Those

of us sticking around for the long haul know how important it is to have good help. Frankly, I'm amazed that the old lady is tackling this." His expression appeared more disparaging than amazed. "It's kind of scary but cool, all at once. I mean, what's the point?"

Funny.

Jace didn't have a whole lot of respect for his biological grandmother, but hearing someone else call her "the old lady" bothered him. "She's my grandmother, Art. And no matter how eccentric she may be, she's hired us to do a job and deserves respect."

The foreman looked from Jace to the house and back. "You're messing with me, right? Because I knew your parents. Remember?"

"My parents adopted me. Gilda is my biological grandmother."

"Well, that's one for the local news, isn't it?" Art folded his arms and braced his legs. "You never knew?"

"Nope."

"In a town that's not known for keeping the lid on anything, folks sure managed to do a good job keeping quiet on this." Art didn't hide his surprise. "Any more surprises up your sleeve, Jace?"

"Two, but nothing you'd believe so we'll leave that for another day. Let's see what you've got."

Art showed him around the buildings. They decided to wait on new gutters until painting was done, and just as Jace was about to head back to his place, Gilda came out the front door wearing another simple cotton dress, the kind with a little white collar and a cinched waist. It was a dress that seemed to come from a long-gone era. "Why are you still here?" He moved forward, concerned because the noise level couldn't be good for an elderly person.

"I had a few things to attend to, and five cats to feed," she told him. She indicated her worn car. "But now I'm ready to go over to Pine Ridge. I'm going to show Corrie how to put up sour cherry jam. It's not something they did in Kentucky, I guess."

"I love sour cherry jam," he said. He wasn't sure why an old-fashioned jam kind of connected him to her, but it did. "It's always been a favorite of mine."

"I gave your mother my recipe a long, long time ago," Gilda told him as she moved toward her car. "She liked learning things and she especially liked learning things about you. Knowing you loved jam and bread from the time you were just a little tyke made her feel like she'd been part of that first year, and that's a good feeling for any mother."

"Except mine." He put the words out there

and let them hang. Art had gone back to work and Gilda paused, her hand on the car door, her eyes down.

"Barbara loved you," she said finally. "As much as she could love anyone, Jason, and I don't know if that's because we failed her or she failed us, and when you get to this age you realize it doesn't really matter and never did. What I do know is that if God offers the chance and time to fix it, you jump on board and do what you can. She didn't have to have you, you know. The law had opened up choices and she could have ended the whole thing and no one would have been the wiser."

Jace stood stock-still as her implication came clear.

"Especially when Lionel shrugged his shoulders and walked off."

The thought of a father turning away from a child was incomprehensible to Jace and the very opposite of how he was raised. "He didn't want me."

"He didn't want much of anything except to be respected but then he had a hard time doing anything respectable so that became a problem." She pressed her lips into a thin line. "He wasn't a terrible person, but he wasn't a strong person, and when your grandfather offered him money to go away, he took it. I'm not saying it was a bad thing to do, but it broke Barbara's heart, thinking he could be bought. She took her college money out of the funds we set up for her and decided she didn't have one drop of interest in being a mother... And that's when I thought of Ivy and Jason." She sighed softly, gazing out, then brought her eyes back to his. "They wanted a baby so badly and thirty years ago there weren't all these specialized clinics to help folks who couldn't have children, so year after year they waited. Hoping. Praying. They'd put in for adoption but babies were scarce." She winced. "When Barbara decided she wanted her freedom, placing you with Ivy and Jason seemed like the right thing to do. I had exactly what they wanted." She said those words softly. So softly.

But Jace heard the truth behind the words. "A dark-skinned baby that wouldn't fit the Hardaway image."

She turned toward him with a look of anguish. Not just everyday sorrow, but true grief. "You always fit my image, Jason. From the very first day. But I will confess that I married a man who wasn't the kindest or best or a believer in anything other than himself and money, so in that way you're correct. You didn't fit *that* Hardaway image. But don't you ever think for one solitary moment that you didn't fit mine. Because you did."

She opened the car door, climbed in and pulled it shut behind her. Then she backed out, leaving him to consider what she'd said.

Easy words now. To pretend she'd cared, that she'd loved him. That she'd gone the distance for him, but the former opulence of the grand old house said that appearances had been important, at least back then.

He moved to the classic barn, climbed up to the loft for a better view and paused.

Idyllic beauty rolled along fields tipping away from the house. From the ground, two decades of growth obscured the view of the land that made up the Hardaway acreage. From here, the rolling fields opened wide with opportunity. Gilda must have rented some of the land out, a smart move. Two mammoth hay fields stretched across the valley. A series of broad paddocks meant for cattle linked far pastures to the nearest barn, but there were twin barns forming an L at the far end of the second paddock. From here he could see the gravel drive, hidden from the road by long years of brush growth, where trailers must have pulled in to load market calves.

The place must have thrived in its day.

A tiny seed of what-if stirred inside him.

Could this place be brought back to life? Could the ranch be restarted?

Does it matter? It's not yours to speculate on.

It wasn't, thought Jace as he snapped a series of pictures with his phone, but he wasn't a fool. He'd sat at Grandpa Middleton's feet when the old man talked about Middleton land. Middleton horses. The Middleton Ranch, gone before Jace was born, but something to aspire to. A few bad years had put the ranch on the market a long time ago, and Jace understood the truth in that. A farming enterprise could sustain some ups and downs, but too many bad years spelled disaster.

But this—

This spread must have been unbelievable in its day, and still Gilda had let the whole thing go to wrack and ruin once her husband died.

A call from the pediatrician's office interrupted his musings. And when he explained why he needed both girls to be seen and evaluated, the nurse offered him an appointment in four days.

He gripped the phone tight. "Four days? You can't get them in sooner?"

"Are they ill, sir?"

"No, they're fine."

"No fever, no injury, nothing out of sorts?"

"Well, if you can conclude that a possible hearing loss isn't out of sorts, then no. I guess not." He sounded snippy. He felt snippy, as if this should be taken much more seriously by the medical community.

She moved the appointment up a day and apologized, which made him feel like a jerk. "Mr. Middleton, we've got to get the records transferred from the clinic so we can see what the twins have had in the way of immunizations and care. To be able to properly assess what's going on, we need to do physicals and bring them up to date in our practice. It's not that Mountain View Pediatrics doesn't share your concern, but we'd be remiss to jump the gun before we have all the facts, and because you've got twins, I need to block out sufficient time for each baby."

He hated that it made perfect sense, and when she gave him a twelve-thirty Thursday appointment time, he realized someone would be missing their lunch break because he'd thrown a mini-fit. "Actually, go back to the Friday date," he told her. "You're right, I'm new at this and more than a little nervous. And let me add that I hate admitting that," he finished.

"If you're sure?"

"Yes. Friday at nine thirty is fine."

He pocketed the phone before he climbed down the loft ladder, then pulled it back out when he reached the ground floor and hit Rosie's number on speed dial. "How are the girls doing?"

She laughed. "So well! Miss Ava has taken a few more steps today, but mostly is crawling and trying to make her way to off-limits places like the stove and the bathroom, while Annie is quite content to amuse herself and watch her sister's antics from a distance."

"How can they be so different?" he asked as he moved to his truck. "They're genetically identical. This makes no sense."

"The body may appear the same, but the soul is unique, is it not?"

He hadn't thought of that. It made perfect sense. "Well, of course they couldn't have the same soul."

"Exactly the truth, which is why science can only do so much. For the rest, we trust in God."

"Thank you, Rosie. I'm heading back to my place to work on the bathroom. Call me if you need me."

"Of course."

He drove back to his parents' house—his house now, his and Justine's—quickly. There was a lot to do in the next week because once they began interior demolition on Gilda's house, he'd be tied there for several months. Even working with a crew of one or two, he wouldn't be setting any speed records, and how would the folks at Pine Ridge hold up if Gilda became a regular visitor?

He cringed but decided to cross that bridge when he came to it. He spotted Melonie's car as he crested the hill a few minutes later. His pulse jumped.

He tamped it right back down. She'd made her position clear, but the moment he spotted her sitting in the shade of the catalpa trees, wearing that ridiculously big hat and tapping away on her laptop, his heart leaped again.

She looked up. Smiled. And when she did, something stirred inside him, an urge to keep right on inspiring those smiles. He crossed the yard as she stood. "Were you able to set something up for the girls?" she asked right off.

His heart thwarted his lame attempts to tamp it down the moment she asked the question. While their job at Hardaway Ranch was huge, nothing mattered more than those babies' well-being. "Friday morning."

"That's the soonest they could see them?" She looked as surprised as he'd felt, but when he explained the nurse's reasoning, she nodded. "That makes sense," she agreed when he was done. Then she indicated the laptop. "I think I've grown too accustomed to instant gratification and quick-moving programs. I have to say that's one of the perks of being up here in the country. Things aren't moving at a breakneck pace."

She turned away to get the laptop. "You found Kentucky to be fast-paced?" The South wasn't exactly known for moving quickly.

She burst out laughing and turned back.

So pretty, with her hair pulled off to one side,

just enough to hide that scar. So bright and engaging. A great smile. The inviting laugh. And skin so soft...so touchable...

He reached a hand to her cheek.

Yes, he'd promised himself to steer clear, but there was no keeping clear of this woman. Her warmth and joy urged him closer, even when common sense scolded him to keep away. "Melonie." He didn't mean for his voice to go all deep and husky. But it did, the moment he felt the warmth of her skin beneath his hand.

She didn't move. She gazed up at him with a softer smile now, but a look that offered permission. Permission he couldn't refuse.

He kissed her. He kissed her long and slow. And she kissed him right back. He held her close, her head tucked against his big, old cowboy-beatin' heart. "I know we're not supposed to do this."

"So why do you suppose we keep right on doing it?" she whispered, but there was amusement in her tone. "Because I'm not going to pretend I don't like it, Jace."

He smiled, his cheek pressed against her hair. "I'd say we like to tempt fate, but we don't."

She shook her head, agreeing.

"Or maybe it's that we're thrown together and proximity is the guiding factor."

"I've been in proximity to a lot of men over

the years, and I can't remember anything remotely like this." She leaned her head back and caught his gaze, which got her kissed again.

"Then maybe it's just meant to be, Melonie. Maybe we'd be downright foolish to fight it."

He felt her smile against the thin cotton of his shirt. "Now, that's a solid pick-up line."

"Or a solemn pledge," he whispered. But then he stepped back firmly. "However, we've got work to do, and I need to read up on kids' hearing disorders later, so what've you got for me? And I promise not to shoot it down too quickly."

She picked up the laptop and set it onto her lap as he settled onto the bench beside her. She showed him a photo of the front of Gilda's house. "We'll keep this the same except for adding this eight-foot window unit here. It's a shame to have a view like that and not exploit it from the house."

He'd noticed that, too. "So we add on this window bay. For both stories?" he asked, surprised, and she nodded.

"It will balance the lines of the house and that way whoever has the master bedroom on the second floor can share the view that we'll have in the living room."

"It's beautiful. And functional," he added.

"Function first, but there's nothing wrong with dolling it up," she told him. She was looking down and when she did, she pushed the hank of hair from her left shoulder, revealing the scar.

He reached up gently. Then ran his finger along the inverted C of the mark.

She turned sharply, and there was no missing the deer-in-the-headlights look she gave him. "Stop that."

He dropped his hand but not his attention. "What happened?"

She huffed a breath, went back to the computer and ignored his question.

Jace Middleton didn't hold well with being ignored. "Tell me." He left the words hanging for a few seconds before he whispered, "Please."

She stared down.

Her jaw went tight, and for just a moment she resembled her uncle when he'd had about enough of people's nonsense. But then she breathed in and out. She lifted the shoulder closest to him in a half shrug. "I went a few rounds with a very big horse when I was eight years old. The horse won."

He leaned forward to catch her eye. "I'm so sorry." The thought of a small child being injured by a huge horse wasn't something he'd ever had to worry about. Now he would.

She looked the other way.

"Hey, don't do that." He reached around and

turned her gently. "I didn't mean to put you on the spot."

"Yet, you did."

"Yes." He waited for her to turn. She didn't. "I asked Lizzie and she said it wasn't her story to tell."

"Old news, Jace. I'd prefer to talk about the future, not the past."

If sadness had a name, it was written in her eyes. Her expression. He recognized that emotion in her face right now, and he longed to make it disappear. "We don't have to say any more about it. Not now. Not ever. But if you ever want to talk, Melonie?" He stroked her cheek, staying clear of the scar. "I'm here."

For just a moment he thought she might give in. Open up.

She didn't. Gazing down, she went to the next page of her prospective designs. "I appreciate the offer."

Give her space. Give her time. Give yourself time to feel your way through all of this.

"When is your sister coming in?"

It was a good change of subject. He'd had some time to get used to this strange turn of events. Justine would be coming face-to-face with the babies and the reality that he wasn't biologically related to her. "Friday night. Then she catches a flight back on Sunday afternoon."

"Well, let's get cracking here. If you can have the girls over here, then Justine has time to absorb all of this without the entire Fitzgerald clan hovering around."

"It is a whole lot busier and noisier than it used to be," he teased, but it was the simple truth. Since Lizzie and Corrie had come to town, the ranch had courted visitors of all kinds, held a beautiful memorial service for Sean Fitzgerald and stirred up emotions in a place that most thought was dead.

Shepherd's Crossing wasn't dead.

Sleeping, maybe, but the Fitzgerald women didn't seem too keen on letting things lay low or stay quiet and he was beginning to think they were just what the town needed.

Chapter Twelve

The paint crew arrived at Jace's house at dawn Thursday morning. They had the house and trim done just in time for a local service to install gleaming white gutters, but when Melonie asked about moving the girls into the house, Jace put her off.

"I'm going to wait until Justine heads back to Seattle," he told her Friday morning as he and Corrie fed the girls.

"Why?" she asked as she sipped her coffee. If she stayed on this side of the wall, maybe the longing to jump in and feed those babies—care for those little girls and their handsome guardian—could be kept in submission.

That worked for about five seconds, and then Ava spotted her and clapped her hands, slopping morning mush all over herself, Jace and the high-chair tray. "Bah!" She reached her arms right out toward Melonie. "Abba abba bah!" And despite Jace's best efforts to keep feeding her, Ava was insistent. She wanted Melonie and that left Melonie no choice. She wet a clean washcloth from the stack Cookie kept on the nearby counter and crossed to the extended table. "You're a mess, schnookums."

Ava grinned and slapped her gooey hand against the tray, splattering all of them again. "Nee Nee!"

"A new word has been added to our extensive vocabulary." Jace swiped goo from his arm and cheek, then kept feeding Annie, who didn't seem nearly as excited to see Melonie.

"I think she's saying your name," Corrie remarked as she helped wipe down a whole list of things that bore the splatter of Ava's enthusiasm. "Melonie. Nee Nee."

"Bah! Nee Nee!" Ava grinned at Melonie, so precious and funny and sweet. Corrie had set the spoon on the tray.

Ava picked it up, stuck it in her mouth, then grinned like a little clown.

"Oh, you are going to be a handful, darling girl." Melonie took Corrie's spot, a seat that brought her right next to Jace, the very man she'd tried to avoid for forty-eight hours—only when you're working a major project with a person, necessity brought proximity, so how on earth was she going to table this attraction?

"Jace?"

They both looked up as Lizzie approached. She held a printout in her right hand. "I've got information on Valencia. Where she is right now, at least."

His jaw tightened, but he nodded. "Thank you. One way or another we've got to make things legal. It would be great if she would sign rights over without issue, but either way we can't leave these babies in limbo. That leaves them with no legal protection if she comes back, and the sheriff said she could be arrested for abandonment if she returns." He took the paper from Lizzie while she made coffee. "I don't want to make a bad situation worse than it already is, but we've got to put the girls' safety first."

He scanned the paper quickly.

Melonie wanted to ask what it said.

She didn't have to.

He held it out to her. "She's in Oregon right now. Near Bend. Should I ask you how you got this information?" He posed the question to Lizzie once she brewed her coffee.

"Probably not."

"I've got the girls' doctor's appointments this morning, then Justine's due to arrive this evening." He drew his eyebrows down. "Who'd have ever thought I'd have to ignore one sister to help the other?"

"Well, Justine's making the effort to be here. To spend time with you and meet her nieces." Melonie stayed practical. "If Lizzie tracked Valencia down once, she'll do it again."

"And who knows? She may stay put there for a while. There are a bunch of hotels there looking for housekeeping help. She's experienced and has a decent track record with her former employer," Lizzie noted.

"The amount of information that comes to your fingertips is mind-boggling and possibly frightening." Melonie handed Ava her sippy cup.

Disenchanted with the option, the baby tossed it to the floor and burst out laughing.

Melonie retrieved it and handed it back.

Ava grinned...and tossed it down again. She was having her own personal game of fetch and Melonie was the pup-in-training.

"You're done." Melonie slipped off the tray, handed it to Corrie and lifted the baby out of the seat. "We don't throw things," she scolded as she re-swabbed Ava's face with a clean, wet cloth. "That's naughty."

Ava's eyes went round.

Her lower lip thrust out and she stared up at Melonie in disbelief, as if her beloved Nee Nee had just delivered a crushing blow.

Then she started crying. Big, breath-shaking tears, about as cute and over-the-top as she could get.

"I made her cry." Melonie looked from Jace to Corrie and back, distressed because this was the last thing she expected. "What do I do? I just made an itty-bitty girl start crying. I didn't mean to," she went on.

"She'll be fine in two minutes," counseled Lizzie. "Show her a shiny object. It will help. I promise."

"Better they cry now than you cry later," added Corrie. "Being naughty might be cute at this age. It is not amusing when babies grow. There is no time like the present to begin that lesson."

"Lessons? They're not even a year old." Jace looked as surprised as Melonie felt.

"Lessons begin the moment they start reaching for the stove. Or a sharp object. Or a doorknob. We begin teaching to keep them safe. We keep teaching so they learn to love knowledge."

"That settles it." Jace grinned at Annie as she blew raspberries through her last bite of Corrie's mush. "I'm taking Corrie home with me. I need her counsel and wisdom to get me through this. At least the first year," he added. "Corrie, what do I have to do to tempt you away from all this?"

"Marry one of my girls," she shot back, and

never even looked over her shoulder. "I am an officially retired nanny," she went on as she rinsed baby dishes in the sink. "But I will never retire from being their mama or a grandma. That's the only way to get my services these days, I'm afraid." The older woman aimed a knowing look at Jace. "But I appreciate the compliment."

"It could be worth it," Lizzie teased. "Like a two-for-one sale at the grocery."

"We'll have to see if Charlotte's available when she arrives." Melonie shot her sister a stern look as she grabbed a handful of tissues. Ava's sobs lessened to whimpers against her shoulder. "I'm taking little Miss Ava to get changed."

Jace's phone rang as she went to the living room. They'd set up a changing station there. Diapers, wipes, onesies and rompers. Jace came into the room as she finished dressing Ava. She stepped away from the changing table and set Ava on the floor. "Your turn."

The first day it had taken him a long time to change the wriggling babies. Not anymore. He got Annie cleaned and dressed in record time, then set her near her sister. "Gilda wants to come to the doctor's office with me."

"It's kind of nice that she wants to be involved, isn't it?" she asked. Then she read his face. "How is that bad?"

He made a face. "Not bad. Awkward. I don't

know what to say to her. What not to say. And I still feel like lashing out irrationally when she harps on the past."

"Perhaps for her it's not harping, but asking forgiveness. And understanding."

"What if I can't understand why they did what they did?"

"That's a self-directed question if ever there was one."

He frowned as the rumble of Gilda's tires crunched across the barnyard gravel. "Why does everything have to get talked to death? Maybe that's a better question. Listen." He put his hand over hers. "I know you've got work to do, but if I absolutely leave you alone to work this afternoon, will you come with us? To the doctor's appointment? Not just because of my grandmother, I'm pretty sure I can handle her, but I could really use your help."

"You don't need me there, Jace." She knew it, and she was pretty sure he knew it, too. Including her in family things like this would only make things harder and, frankly, they were hard enough already.

She stood to go.

Ava grabbed her ankle. And her heart. "Nee?" She grabbed hold of Melonie's other leg and stared up, imploring. "Nee?"

"She is saying your name." Jace looked at Ava

with such a look of pride that Melonie's heart went soft all over again. "How cute is that?"

"Nee." Ava patted Melonie's leg, then raised her arms up.

"We both want you to come, Melonie."

How could she resist that? Maybe she was foolish to tie all her dreams to a what-if life down South. What if she dared to transfer her hopes and dreams to the forest-rimmed valley of western Idaho?

Ava leaned her head against Melonie's leg, as if hugging her. She lifted the baby and kissed her soft cheek. "If you promise to give me work time this afternoon…"

Jace smiled. "My word of honor."

What a delight that she could actually trust his word. She lifted the diaper bag he'd packed earlier.

He had Annie in one arm.

She held Ava.

And when he reached over to take the bag from her shoulder, a new thought blossomed. Of raising these two girls together. Here, in the mountain-rimmed valley.

Are you crazy?

She felt a little crazy when she looked up at Jace and matched his smile. And when his deepened, her heart quickened, a ridiculous and absolutely marvelous reaction.

"Best get going." Gilda was at the base of the porch stairs, impatient. "We don't want to keep the doctor waiting."

"You're right," said Jace. "We don't want to be rude."

"Are they warm enough?" Gilda's voice lost a grain of harshness when she talked about the babies.

Melonie answered as she wrestled Ava into her seat. "If not, she will be," she muttered. "The struggle is real."

"And little Annie goes right in." Gilda seemed surprised, and Melonie couldn't blame her.

"The same but different, right?"

"I guess." Gilda seemed flustered. She eyed the vehicle, then her car.

"You ride with Jace. I'll follow along."

"You don't mind? I don't go driving into the city much."

"Happy to do it."

She opened the door for Gilda. The old woman climbed in and pulled her seat belt into place.

She didn't dare look at Jace.

She could have had Gilda ride with her, but learning to be family around these girls was part of the point, wasn't it?

Her phone rang as she followed them out of the driveway. She hit the Bluetooth connection when she recognized the name of her former coworker. "Ezra, hey. How are things going? Have you found a job yet?" Ezra Jones had been her photographer and site director for the magazine. He'd staged the looks, taken the shots and organized the production of her *Shoestring Southern Charm* pilot videos six months ago. When the magazine folded, so did his job.

"Possibly. I might have found *us* a job."

She'd pulled out of the driveway but paused. "Us?"

"I'll give you the details. I'm heading your way."

"You're coming here?"

"Kentucky is blazing hot and I wanted to go over a few things with you. Get your opinion. You don't mind, do you?"

Ezra had been her friend for years. "Of course not. Come on up and bring your cameras. There is a wild and rustic beauty up here. Not low-key, sweet-tea serenity like we have in the South. But beautiful."

"I'll let you know when I get close."

"You're going to leave me hanging?" she asked as she navigated the next turn.

"Temporarily. I'm working out details. Car phone connections are amazing things."

"Talk to you soon." She disconnected the call, but there wasn't a lot of time to ponder his meaning. Ezra thought outside the box, 24/7. He was a concept guy, who looked beyond the everyday, and he'd end up somewhere, doing great things. She knew that because he had the talent and the drive to see it through. They'd made a great team.

A job for us...

And yet he knew she had to be here for a year.

She reviewed her options for Gilda's house. Her palms itched as she considered the magnitude of this project. She'd have Ezra grab pictures of the "before." She'd sent him a few when she and Jace made the agreement with Gilda, and he'd sent back a one-word answer. *Wow.*

Wow was right, but as she'd gotten to know Gilda, and sensed the longing to make things right, the house design became more than a massive makeover.

It became a mission.

Chapter Thirteen

Annie didn't need help.

Ava did.

"I'm going to send you to a specialist near Boise," the pediatrician told them midmorning. "My guess is they'll recommend putting tubes in Ava's ears."

"Tubes for what?" Gilda drew her eyebrows tight, and when she did that, the word *formidable* came to Jace's mind. "What do tubes do and why does she need them?"

The doctor didn't take offense. Jace guessed she'd worked with frightened grandparents before. She pulled out a chart while the twins batted small plastic balls around the carpeted floor of a small meeting room. "She's got fluid buildup in her right ear. I looked at the clinic records and saw she'd been treated for three ear infections in five months."

"Her caregiver told us that she's had recurring colds and light fevers."

"So it's even possible that she's had a couple of undiagnosed issues. For some kids, it's no big deal. For others, like Ava, the chronic ear infections leave a fluid buildup and dull hearing. It is usually reversible with the tubes and maturation, but I'll let the ENT doctor go into that detail. We'll set up the appointment for next week, and they'll take it from here."

"Should we do both?" asked Gilda. Melonie stayed quiet. She'd taken a seat on the floor and let the girls crawl all over her, keeping them happy while Jace, Gilda and the physician talked.

"It's always curious when identical twins show differences like this, isn't it?"

Gilda nodded.

"Annie's not showing any signs of problems, and her newborn screening and this hearing screening are both normal. I'd chalk this up to normal variances. When you're talking babies and narrow passageways, growth is often our best friend. A more open passage allows the body to get rid of bacteria and viruses faster. Faster healing, fewer problems."

"They don't have insurance," Gilda spouted. "But I'll pay for what needs doing."

"Wonderful." The doctor smiled at her, and

Gilda seemed to physically relax. "You're the great-grandmother, correct?"

She nodded.

"And you're the uncle seeking guardianship?"

"I am."

The doctor leaned forward. "Something for you to consider. If the specialist's office questions guardianship, they probably have to refuse treatment."

Jace wasn't just surprised by that. He was shocked. In the local towns, no one refused Gilda Hardaway anything. It simply wasn't done. "What?"

The doctor explained her meaning in a matter-of-fact manner. "They'll need parental signatures to proceed. Or, if the girls become wards of the state, then they'll need the Human Services office to okay the surgical procedure."

"I have the means to pay," Gilda insisted. "And my great-granddaughters aren't wards of anything. They're family!"

The doctor sent her a sympathetic look. "And they're blessed to have so many people invested in their outcome, but the specialist will need to have a legal guardian approve treatment."

"What if we had an emergency and needed treatment?" Jace asked. He'd never considered they might refuse to help the girls.

"In an emergency situation, the need to treat

outweighs everything. But it's still a sticking point that should be rectified ASAP. Will your guardianship be approved soon?"

Jace scrubbed his hand against the nape of his neck. "That's uncertain."

"Well, my advice is to get that done quickly," she said, standing. "They'll ask, and you don't want to be falsifying records. It's not about who's caring for the kids," she assured Jace in a kind voice. "It's about legal recourse, and hospitals are pretty picky about it. You might want to get the legal ends tied up quickly."

There was no quick way to fix this unless Valencia signed off. "I'll get right on it."

"Good." She shook his hand and referred them to the front desk, where an efficient office manager took care of setting up the appointment for the specialist in two weeks. Which meant he needed to get to Bend with legal papers and get Valencia to sign off before then.

What if she didn't?

He didn't dare think that way, because when Annie clutched his neck and blew raspberry kisses along his cheek, her laughter clinched the deal. How could he not take a chance on them? And did his sister care?

There was only one way to find out.

They tucked the girls into the car seats and he placed a call to Mack Grayson. Mack was a cowboy by birth and a lawyer by education, the perfect guy to help local ranchers and business owners. He left Mack a voice mail, then headed back toward Shepherd's Crossing.

A few weeks ago he'd been lamenting too much time on his hands. That wasn't the problem any longer. Now he'd have to figure out getting to Bend, finishing his house, working with the demolition crew on Gilda's place, caring for two children and having time with Justine over the next couple of days.

"Do you want me to go to Oregon? I can take the train over."

Gilda's raspy voice interrupted his running thoughts.

"To see Valencia?" That might be the worst idea ever. Or the best. How would he know? But Gilda wasn't in great health, so he nixed the idea. He spoke gently because he didn't want to hurt the old woman's feelings. "I appreciate the offer, but I'd prefer to go myself. What I'd really like, if you have the time—" he angled a quick glance her way "—is if you'd help with the babies while I'm gone. It's a lot for Rosie to handle and I'd feel better knowing they're having some Gee Gee time. I want them to know their family, as silly as that might sound at their age."

"Not silly at all." She didn't sound so raspy right now. "You knew your mom and me real well, Jason. By this age you'd figured out how to wrap me right around your finger with those big brown eyes and that beautiful smile." Eyes down, she fiddled with her purse strap as she spoke. Her voice had gone soft, talking about him. Now it hiked up once more, as if she was excited about the girls. "Getting to know these two will be an absolute pleasure."

She sounded genuinely excited.

And yet when his mother abandoned ship, his grandmother didn't step in to raise him. Why?

Try as he would, he couldn't understand her decision. He couldn't imagine giving the twins away to someone or walking away from them. And that only made him wonder how parents justified such a choice?

A return call from Mack interrupted his thoughts. "Mack, I need some legal help and I need it fast. Can I come by today?"

"I'm making a house call to Carrington Acres in about an hour," Mack told him. "How about if I swing by your place after that?"

That would give him enough time to get the girls back to Rosie's and make the short drive to his house. "That works. See you shortly." He hung up as he turned down the Pine Ridge Ranch driveway.

"Is Grayson that young lawyer from Council?" Gilda asked.

"That's him."

"His daddy was one of those Grayson boys from up in the hills."

Jace wondered if there was a point to the statement. There usually was…eventually.

"I knew his grandfather. We kept company for a while when we were young."

Well, that was a surprise. "You and Mack's grandfather?"

She pressed her lips into a thin line. "I was young. My parents owned the original mercantile on Main Street and then bought a couple of other businesses as well."

He'd known the town had a rich history, but the sadness of losing the Middleton Ranch had made Shepherd's Crossing history verboten in their house. So he knew *of* it, but not much about it.

"I never did without, and I thought that was the reason I was happy." She rolled her eyes as they drew up to Rosie's turnoff. "The foolishness of youth, I guess. So when Richard Hardaway showed interest, I showed interest right back because he was already on his way to a bright future and I knew I'd want for nothing." She twisted her fingers, restless. "Life might have been very different if I'd made other choices, but then I wouldn't have you. Or these precious girls. So maybe things work out in their own way after all."

He had no idea what she meant, and she did like to ramble, but if she was talking regret, then, yeah. He had a few. But more joy than regret overall. Even with the craziness of this new family situation.

He dropped Gilda and the girls off at Pine Ridge, then hurried back to his house. Justine would be arriving that evening. He wanted to spend time with her, but with the doctor's news, maybe he didn't have that time to spare.

Melonie had texted him that she was going straight to his house to work, but when he pulled into the drive, she wasn't there.

He started to text her when her SUV rolled into the short driveway. She parked next to him, climbed out and handed him a deli bag. "Sandwiches. And more of that cowboy blend coffee. I saw you were getting low and figured I'd grab some while we were in the city."

He didn't need more reasons to fall for this woman, but thoughtfulness and kindness added to the growing list. Food and coffee. So simple, but crazy appreciated.

She saw. She acted. Those were great assets in business, but he realized they were also wonderful in everyday life. That get-it-done mindset his parents had embraced.

Camryn hadn't been like that. He realized that after she dumped him, that her life wasn't structured around others. It revolved around her. In retrospect she'd done him a favor, leaving him.

Melonie was an amazing woman with her own list of hopes and dreams. Did he dare take the risk, knowing her plans?

One look at her face told him it was already too late. He grabbed a pair of sodas from the fridge and brought them to the table. "Can I leave the girls at the ranch while I track down their mother in Oregon?"

"Of course. I just assumed that's what we'd do." She unwrapped her sandwich, then surprised him by reaching for his hand to say grace. Head bowed, she talked to God like they were old friends.

"Lord, we thank You for this food. Simple fare, the best kind there is. And, Lord, we ask You to bless Jace with wisdom about the babies, about their mother. He's in an unexpected place, God, and he could use Your guiding hand. Amen."

"That was sweet, Mel."

She focused on food, not compliments. Then she waved toward the laptop. "I've got a huge amount of work to do the next five days, and you're almost done here, which keeps you on track. But you weren't planning on spending a couple of days in Bend, I expect."

"I wasn't," he admitted. "But I can't leave this hanging, and if we sue for abandonment, then she's got some kind of official record to her name. I don't want to make trouble for anyone. But I need to make things right. And keep the girls safe."

A knock sounded on the door, but Mack didn't wait for an invitation. He walked right in, spotted Melonie and swiped his hat off mighty quick. And if the look of appreciation in his eyes got any brighter, Jace might have to knock some sense into him, and that would be a shame because they'd been friends a long time. "Mack, you hungry? Melonie grabbed sandwiches and there's plenty."

"I just ate, thanks, and you must be Melonie Fitzgerald." Mack extended his hand. "I'm the one who sent you the copy of your uncle's will."

"I remember. Thank you." She stood and shook his hand. "I'm going to use the office for work while you two sort out the contract and the relinquishment papers."

Mack made himself coffee while Jason talked, and when he got done, Mack was stirring half the sugar bowl into his cup. He tasted it, then brought it to the table. "The relinquishment papers are a simple draw-up. That's ironic, right?"

He asked Jace. "I can polish those a whole lot faster than the house contract and that's a sorry commentary of today's world. Giving over custodial rights is a clear and simple matter. I'll have that to you by tomorrow morning. The house contract can go either way," he went on as he retrieved a notepad from his Western-tooled leather case. "We keep it precise and notate every little thing, or we keep it more general and you work within boundaries."

"The latter. I don't think my grandmother knows what she wants, but she sure knows what she doesn't want. A mess of a house and yard anymore."

"I'll have the house papers to you midweek. Does that give you time to start demolition? You don't want to jump into that until the contract is ready and signed."

"By Wednesday, yes. I can be done here and back from Bend."

"Then I'll make sure you have them by Tuesday so all parties are covered before you go all out."

Jace stood and shook Mack's hand. "Thank you. I'm grateful."

"The house looks great, Jace." Mack slipped the notepad into the bag once he stood. "The exterior, the gardens, the yard."

"It took two babies to light a fire under me to

update. I don't know what I was waiting for, but it's nearly done now."

"And a huge project awaits." Mack faced him when they got outdoors. He glanced toward the house. "Is she up for it?" he asked.

"Over-the-moon to be able to show her stuff."

"What about you?" Mack's expression turned serious. "This had to hit hard, Jace. We've been friends a long time. But hey, if you don't want to talk about it—"

He didn't. And he did. He grimaced. "A lot to get used to, but then I look around and realize that drama follows lots of families. I just never associated it with mine."

"I know. Your mom and dad were the best. They were sure good to me." He clapped a hand on Jace's shoulder. "I'm out. I'll see you Tuesday."

"Thanks, Mack."

Mack offered a no-thanks-needed wave as he climbed into his car. By the time Justine pulled into the driveway later that afternoon, the bathroom was complete and the floor was ready for refinishing. The interior paint crew would come by on Monday to freshen up the living areas with fresh coats of cream-colored paint.

Melonie had gone back to the ranch. When he asked her to stay, she'd gripped his hand gently. "You need time to talk to your sister alone.

Then bring her over. Don't make it too late or the girls will be cranky and tired. Cookie's got barbecue going and Corrie's made a bunch of sides to feed us through the weekend. That way we can relax with the girls while you're gone."

She was stepping up to the plate big-time. He knew she needed time to plot out rooms. The Hardaway house wasn't a typical box-style home. The architectural integrity of it needed to be respected, even when changed.

"Corrie has assured me that I'll have time to work."

"Did I look that worried?" He wasn't a worrier by nature. But then, he'd never been a parent before.

"Concerned," she told him. She grabbed her bag and hurried toward the door. "I'm expecting a phone call on some materials and it's easier to pick it up uninterrupted in the car. See you tonight."

He worked nonstop until he heard the crunch of Justine's tires in the driveway.

He didn't wait for her to come in.

He walked out to meet her, and when she climbed out of the car, she took one look around the beautifully reclaimed gardens and burst into tears.

And when Jace pulled his little sister into his arms—and felt her sob against his chest—emotions put a stranglehold on him, too. They'd cried at two graves in the past five years, but they had each other. They still did…and now, so much more.

Justine Middleton wasn't just lovely, Melonie realized when Jace and his sister pulled into the ranch later that day.

She carried herself with a quiet dignity, like her big brother. And when she climbed out of her car and spotted the girls in the double stroller, she went straight down to their level instantly. "Oh, my word, Jace, they're beautiful. And they really are babies!"

Jace aimed a dumbfounded look down. "I may have mentioned that. And I sent pictures, sis." He shifted his attention to Melonie and Corrie, behind the stroller. "So this is my sister, Justine, aka Captain Obvious."

"Hey." She looked up at Melonie and Corrie, smiling. "He sent pictures, yes, but the reality is a thousand times better." She stood and stepped back when Ava stuck out a quivering lower lip, but extended her hand. "It's so nice to meet you both, and thank you for helping Jace figure all this out."

"Well, it's mostly me," growled a distinctly male voice from the porch.

Justine spun around, laughed and dashed up the steps. "Heath!"

"Hey, kid." Heath hugged her, and when he stopped, he kept an arm draped loosely around her shoulders. "Glad you could sneak away for the weekend. Welcome home, brat. We want to hear your plans while you're here. What's in store for little Justine Middleton when the internship ends?"

She gazed up, indecisive. "I don't know," she told him. She directed a sincere smile toward the stroller. "I thought I did, but this is a game-changer."

"It's not," said Jace from his spot in the driveway. "I've got this. You've got a career to build and a life to lead, Jus. Don't make me go all bigbrother on you."

She laughed, and Melonie liked her more because of it. "As if. We've got lots to sort out and I'm taking time to do it," she told him. "I'm putting it in God's hands and I intend to get to know these babies all weekend. If that's all right?" She looked from Heath to Melonie and back. "Jace explained that he's leaving to track down their mother."

"It's more than all right," Heath told her. "We've never had the pleasure of this much female company on the ranch. It's been real nice for us cowboys."

"True words." Jace tipped that black cowboy hat slightly, but when Annie started to fuss, he called Justine back down. "Let's take the girls for a walk. We'll hear the bell when Cookie rings it."

Melonie began to back off.

Jace didn't let her. "I meant all of us."

"Except me," Corrie told them. "I'm needed in the kitchen." She climbed the stairs quickly. "Miss Justine, I'm Corrie Satterly."

Justine's eyes lit up when she heard the distinct Southern accent.

"It's a pleasure to make your acquaintance."

"And yours." Justine came back down the stairs.

"And I'm Melonie Fitzgerald," Melonie added as they began strolling.

"The one who redesigned our house?"

Please don't let her hate me for changing things... Melonie winced slightly. "That's me. I know it was a surprise to come home to. *Another* surprise," she added.

"I love it."

Melonie's heart began beating again.

"Jace didn't want to change a thing, and once you get to know him you realize that he's rock solid in a lot of ways, and not embracing change is only one of many. But Mom had put some changes on hold to help pay for my education.

In a way, you guys have made her dreams come true. I love the new open layout. And the updated bathroom is a huge plus," she laughed.

"I've been handed my share of changes lately," Jace reminded her.

"And you're adjusting brilliantly," Justine teased. "Uh-oh. Someone's unhappy."

Melonie peeked around front of the stroller. Ava was sitting back, content, watching the world.

Annie needed a clean diaper. "Bad timing, little one." They paused the stroller and she lifted Annie out. "I'll walk her back and change her. By then it should be suppertime."

"We'll turn around shortly. Or now," he decided when the porch bell sang out.

"I've always loved this place. This town." Justine smiled at Annie, then Melonie, and when the baby smiled back at her, she posed a question. "Is it normal for them to be this easygoing with so many people?"

Jace shrugged. "Maybe easygoing natures. Maybe being cared for by multiple people. And—" He stopped as Gilda came out of the house. She posted a hand to her forehead, looking for them.

"That's your grandmother."

Jace hated that Justine used words he wouldn't use himself, but it would sound crazy to say so.

"Mrs. Hardaway. Well, Gilda now. Since we're working together."

His sister sent him a sharp look. "I hope you're not playing judge and jury on whatever went on back then, Jason."

He frowned deliberately. At the name? Or her words?

"I've studied enough science to understand that human nature isn't dictated by science but by emotion. She had the guts to come to you, explain everything and beg for help. That couldn't have been easy for a proud woman like her."

"Pride goeth before the fall," he muttered.

Justine rolled her eyes. "And that could mean that lack of pride in one's endeavors brought the fall."

"Or that a prideful spirit is destined to fail."

"Will she be here this weekend?"

"Yes." Melonie kept her voice soft as they drew closer. "They're doing her roofs right now, a complete tear-off and replacement, and that's far too much noise and confusion for an elderly person."

"And she wants to help with the girls. She's surprisingly good at it," he added.

"Then we'll get to know one another over the next couple of days."

"Melonie." Gilda moved to the edge of the porch steps as they climbed up from below. "I know you're busy, and I know you've got a lot on your plate, but I want you to go to Oregon with Jace."

"Except I need to be here to help with the girls and work on your house plans."

"Corrie and I will be here, Rosie's available as needed and while Lizzie is busy with horses this weekend, we can call her on backup. And if Jason's sister is here, I think we've got this covered." She paused, as if picking her words. "To the best of my knowledge, Valencia knows nothing of Jason. I don't think her adoptive mother knew about him, and there was no one to fill her in."

Jace had been lifting Ava out of the stroller. He paused with her in his arms. "You think I'll make her nervous."

"Not nervous. But will she believe you, Jason? Even with my letter?" Gilda frowned in concern. "If we had time to get everything checked out to prove things, that would be one thing."

"You mean like DNA testing." Justine looked from Gilda to Jace. "I'm Justine, Mrs. Hardaway. Jace's sister."

Then Gilda did something out of character. She reached right out and hugged Jace's sister. "It is a pleasure to meet Ivy Middleton's other child," she whispered. "Your mother and father were very dear to me. Very dear."

"They were special people. Jace." She turned toward Jace as he climbed the porch stairs. "I think Mrs. Hardaway is right."

"That I need someone else there? To lessen the blow of a dark-skinned brother?"

"I don't think that will be a blow at all," Gilda argued, and now he stopped again, confused. "But she hasn't met you. It's not like Rosie showing up, or Harve or Heath. She knew all those people. You're a virtual stranger, and I'd suggest Rosie or me going, but Rosie's got a nursing baby and I'm not up for a trip like that. I won't push it," she finished and folded her hands. "I simply think it would be a good idea."

Chapter Fourteen

He hated that his grandmother was right, Jace realized the next day.

He'd never thought about how things might appear to Valencia, because he had the birth certificate and the letter from Gilda explaining things. But why would Valencia willingly sign over her daughters to a stranger, even if that stranger was her half brother? No one in their right mind would do that. Having Melonie along provided a buffer and an opportunity to know her better. That would work except she was busily developing ideas for the old mansion for most of the trip they embarked on the next day.

"Are we close?" she asked as he took a turn-off toward Bend.

"Yes. Do you want to eat first? Or go straight to the inn where she's been working?"

"The inn," she told him. "I'm not sure how

this will all go down and I'm way too nervous to eat."

"And yet you've been working straight through."

"Nerves can't stop production," she told him as she closed the notebook. "My grandpa taught me that. He said there were many times when you did what you had to do, hating it all the while, but you just hunker down and do it. It made sense. And besides, this was the attic rooms and the second floor. Not much scope for the imagination there, but good clean lines to make the building inspector happy."

He spotted the inn's name up ahead. His heart beat louder in his chest, as he pulled into the inn's parking lot. "We're here."

Lizzie hadn't found an address for Valencia. Just a workplace. And he didn't want to do anything to get her fired from her job. But the thought of little Ava, needing medical help and unable to get it, spurred him forward.

He approached the front desk. The clerk looked up, met his gaze and smiled. But when he withdrew a picture of Valencia that Rosie had taken two months before, the smile disappeared and the clerk drew back slightly. "Sir, I'm sorry. I can't answer questions of a personal nature about anyone."

Undeterred, he still proffered the photograph. "This is my sister. She's not in any trouble, I just wanted to connect with her. We were told she works here."

The desk clerk stared him down and reiterated her statement. "I am not allowed to answer questions of a personal nature about anyone. Guest or employee."

Melonie moved forward. "I actually commend you on following the rules," she said. When the woman still appeared suspicious, Melonie withdrew paper from her bag and began to write. "Too many people disregard rules." She spoke as she scribbled a quick note. "They think they know better, but some rules exist to keep people safe." She folded the paper in quarters. "We're here on family business and I honestly don't know how much she'd be comfortable sharing. The name we know her by is Valencia Garcia. Some folks call her Val or Valerie. If she's here, please pass this on to her. We're in town briefly and it's important or we wouldn't have made the six-hour drive. Do you have grandparents?" she asked.

The clerk nodded.

Melonie added a copy of Gilda's note to the folded letter. "This is from the biological grandmother she never knew. She's not in the best of health and we offered to make this trip on her behalf."

She turned and started walking away.

Jace hesitated, torn. They'd come all this way to leave a couple of notes on a desk? Right now he figured the US Postal Service would have been a lot quicker and easier.

He caught up with Melonie just outside the door. "We're leaving?"

"We're going across the road to have coffee. And lunch. I'm starving, aren't you?"

"Now you're hungry?"

She leaned against the door. "For a patient man, you sure are impatient right now. Give her time to get the note. Read it. Think about it. Have you ever had to work a job like this? Tucked in a building all day, away from the sunshine and the breeze, cleaning rooms and scrubbing toilets?"

Of course he hadn't.

"Let's not cost her the job she's found. Let's wait and see what she says. If she comes over on her lunch break."

"You told her we'd be across the street?"

"I did. What I didn't tell her is that we've got rooms booked in this hotel for tonight."

He'd done that in case they couldn't see her. Or if she wasn't there. "She might not be here. I mean here, as in Bend. She might have moved on."

"Then we keep looking. But Lizzie seemed

pretty sure of herself, and I've learned to never second-guess things with my sister."

They drove across the street, ordered coffee and lunch and twenty minutes later, Valencia Garcia walked in the door.

She glanced around the room, puzzled.

Jace got up and started toward her. "Valencia?"

His appearance only deepened her look of question.

He stopped shy of her and extended his hand. He'd come here, unsure what to say.

When he met her eyes, his heart softened. He'd seen lost puppies look more trusting than this woman. "I'm your brother. Jason Middleton. I was adopted by one family and you were adopted by another."

She stared at him, then shot a glance to Melonie.

Melonie put her hands up in surrender. "I'm just moral support. Although I am totally in love with your daughters. Who are both fine, by the way. Mostly."

"Mostly?" Valencia looked from her to Jace quickly. "Is something wrong with them? What is it?"

"Do you have time to sit a minute? Have lunch with us?"

"No, my break is short and I'm new here. I

don't want to mess this up, they've been very good to me. It probably doesn't seem like much of a job to most, but I do it well. And that means something."

"Of course it does. Coffee?"

"Yes, thanks." She took a seat while Melonie ordered the coffee from the café side of the restaurant. Once she sat, she faced Jace. "Are they all right? The girls?"

"Yes and no. Ava's got a hearing problem from so many ear infections and they're going to put tiny tubes in her ears. But the doctor told me they won't let me sign off because I'm not a legal guardian."

Valencia put her head in her hands. "How are you involved in this? I thought that Rosie or maybe Heath would feel sorry for the girls and take them. They're such good people, I knew they'd never let them go."

"Except that's what they'd have to do, and what we'll have to do if you don't relinquish custody of them. No court is going to award their great-grandmother custody at her age, your mother has moved to Florida and I'm not technically part of the family. It's a legal mess that can get cleared up easily with a few official papers."

She winced. Because she needed to let them go? Or because the girls were in danger of becoming wards of the state? He didn't know.

"Gilda approached me a few weeks ago. Right after you left."

"The woman who says she's my grandmother." She lifted Gilda's note.

"Her story checks out, and she asked for my help."

"You're a cowboy. How's a cowboy going to raise two little girls? This wasn't what I wanted to happen. This is wrong. All wrong."

He gave her a minute to compose herself before he spoke. "Their great-grandmother asked me to raise them. She was the one who found my parents for me, my adoptive parents. She's got a good eye for people who love children, but more importantly, she sees all the mistakes of the past and wants to help fix them."

"Is she the skinny old woman who wears her hair up all the time? Kind of frail and bossy?"

He couldn't have described her better. "That's her."

"She came to Rosie's a few times. I saw her there."

"She knew who you were. You didn't know her."

"Why didn't she help then? Why couldn't she have coughed up some of that old money and given me a handout? Or a hand up? She couldn't be bothered then, when I was on my last dime and my mother was trash-talking my name all over the place. Maybe then—" She ducked her chin. Eyes down, her hands clenched. She looked angry and lost and forgotten…

But then she took a breath. A deep one. And her hand came up to a small silver cross hanging from a chain around her neck. And when she took another deep breath, she raised her gaze to his. "I'm sorry."

He waited, unsure what to say.

"I know I'm not right for them." She fingered the cross, restive. "I've known it for a while. I get mad too easy. Frustrated with things, when they don't go my way, and then I don't think straight. I'm trying to do better, but I can't seem to focus on keeping myself calm and taking care of two little girls who need constant attention. They shouldn't be with someone who resents spending time with them. They should be with someone like Rosie, who dotes on children. Maybe motherhood's not my deal—"

"But you had them, Valencia." Melonie interrupted her with that poignant fact. "You had other choices. It takes a woman of courage to make the choice you did."

"I didn't feel all that brave," she admitted. "Mostly sick. And tired. And when the clinic gave me options, I walked right out. I was the only chance the girls had. Babies get a one-shot deal, right?"

Melonie and Jace both nodded.

"So the old lady didn't offer to help, and that was probably because she was right about me. About me not being best for the girls, but I already knew that. So why shouldn't she be right about you?"

Jace read the pain in her eyes.

"She wants to help." When Valencia frowned, he pressed on. "She sent along a check for you." He set Gilda's check on the table.

"To buy me off?"

He shook his head instantly. "No. To assuage the guilt of not acknowledging her family when she had the chance. She's old and not in the greatest health and would love to hear from you. But I understand how that's not the easiest thing to do right now." He slid the check toward her and was glad when she slipped it into her pocket. "It's up to you what you do with it, but she sends it with a sincere heart, Valencia."

"Val. Please. I like Val better." She gazed down for long, drawn seconds as if the weight of the world hung on her shoulders. Then she raised her head and extended her hand. "Do you have the necessary papers with you?"

He withdrew the legal forms from the side of Melonie's computer satchel and handed them over. "A local lawyer drew them up."

She didn't read them.

She scanned them, then signed where indicated. And when she was done, she stood and faced them. "I've got to get back to work."

She turned to leave. Then she paused. Her hand was on the back of the chair. The knuckles strained white against the honey maple wood.

Jace stood, too. "Do you want me to keep you updated, Val? Send you pictures? Keep you in the loop?"

The tight hand said more than her short words. It said how hard it was to let go of something so wonderfully precious...even for their own good. "No." She stood there, facing away, silent. Then she turned slightly and her words hit home with Jace. "Not because I don't love them," she said softly. "But because I do."

She left without a backward glance, and when she cleared the door, Melonie put in a call to cancel their hotel reservations.

Five minutes later they were back in his car, heading east, with the signed papers tucked in her bag.

The girls would be safe. Val would bear no legal problems because of her decision to leave them at Rosie's.

And he...

He swallowed hard because up to this point it had all seemed a little surreal.

He had just become a father.

* * *

While driving back to Shepherd's Crossing, Jace called Mack to file for a court hearing to approve the change of guardianship legally and file adoption papers.

Then he called Justine.

Next was Gilda, letting her know how things went. Despite the slight quiver in her voice, she sounded strong, as if getting things done was having a positive effect.

Melonie dozed off on the way back. He let her sleep, thinking how sweet she looked. How lovely. Wondering what it would be like to have her share this crazy new life with him. With those girls. Sure, she had big plans and dreams, but maybe he and the girls could become her plan. Her dream. She fit with him. Not just as a designer and a builder who would love to run a working ranch, like his grandfather before him. Both grandfathers, he realized.

Melonie inspired him to reach higher. Try harder. Go the distance.

To be a better man.

She touched his heart and soul in a way that had never happened before. So maybe…

He pulled into the Pine Ridge Ranch driveway as he made plans.

Melonie stirred and stretched, then she saw

the house and the time and her eyes went wide. "I slept for two hours?"

"You did. And you didn't snore once."

She smiled at him and that smile set his heart tripping over itself to beat harder. Faster. "Good to know. I—" She paused as a figure stepped down the house steps. Then she laughed, undid her seat belt and was out of the car like a shot. "Ezra!"

The man—a little older than Jace, and square-built—grabbed her in a hug and spun her around. "We got it!" he said, over and over. "I knew we would if we found the right people, Mel, and I wasn't going to stop trying, because you deserve this. All that hard work, all that effort, I wasn't about to let that fall apart for a little thing like geography. You are now the soon-to-be star of *Shoestring Charm*. Just what you always wanted. And I was glad to be the guy who delivered it to you!"

Melonie gave this Ezra guy a kiss on the cheek, and almost squealed for joy. "I can't believe you managed to pull this off." Then she hugged the guy—really hugged him—and the happiness in her face when she turned Jace's way shined the light of truth.

He had no right to steal her hopes. Her dreams. Whoever this guy was, he'd gone the distance for her. He'd done whatever it took to give her the shot she wanted.

Jace didn't have that ability.

He didn't care about renovation shows or fame or fortune. Simple country cowboy was his claim to fame, meager as that was.

He faked a smile, shook the guy's hand, then went inside to tuck the girls into bed. He'd already been away from them too long.

He settled the twins with Corrie and Justine's help, and when they were sound asleep, Corrie poured tall glasses of sweet tea for both Middletons. In a motherly fashion, she shooed them onto the porch. "I'll clean up the toys in here. You two, go. Talk. Figure things out." And when he and Justine settled onto one of the porch swings, he could make out the faint outline of Melonie and her friend, walking and talking in the fading light.

His family was here and that's where he belonged. He knew it. And he was pretty sure Melonie knew it, too.

And it didn't seem to matter nearly as much to her as it did to him.

Chapter Fifteen

"I thought I'd be in time to help get the girls ready for church, but you guys are a step ahead of me," Melonie said as she smiled at Justine and Jace the next morning. "They look wonderful. Do you want me to ride with you? Help with them?" She turned toward Jace.

He didn't look up. Didn't acknowledge her presence at all, actually. He shook his head. "We've got it, thanks. And thanks for the ride-along yesterday, Mel. I really appreciated it."

He said it like you'd thank anyone, not someone you'd kissed several times in the past week.

He said it like she was a casual friend. Worth a nod. Nothing more.

Ava turned her way, arms up, imploring Melonie to cuddle her.

Jace intercepted her smoothly. "Gotta go, little one." He strode through the living room, through the door and down the steps without a backward glance.

Justine reached for Annie and she went willingly, babbling baby sounds. So sweet. So dear.

They settled the twins into the car, then Jace drove off, toward town. The little church had no pastor right now, so area folks took turns leading services. It was a sweet thing to do in a bind.

But Jace's attitude, seeing him drive off without even a backward glance, put her back up. She was done with not being good enough. Done trying to impress the men in her life and falling short.

Standing there, she realized that she wasn't the one falling short.

It was them. And between Uncle Sean's generosity and Ezra's industry, she didn't have to impress anyone anymore, because Ezra's good news proved she already had.

In church, she sat with her family. Prayed with them. And when folks were exclaiming to Jace and Justine about the girls after the service, she quietly left the church and headed back to the ranch.

No one got to brush her off. Not now. Not ever again.

She buried herself in the stable apartment, working on the first-floor plans for Gilda's house, and when Ezra came by midday, she took him to the Hardaway house so he could meet Gilda and ask permission to film there.

If Gilda refused, it would be a blow, but not a crushing blow because Shepherd's Crossing was ripe with makeover opportunities. She'd had one crushing blow already that day, when Jace shrugged her off as unimportant.

Anything else would be easy, compared to that.

Jace didn't have to worry about how to keep his distance from Melonie.

She did it for him, and that was an unexpected burr beneath his saddle for the following week. Justine had gone back to the West Coast and he felt more assured about his guardian status since the trip to Bend, but his personal status had crashed and burned. That's what he needed, right? To create distance from a woman bound for cable TV glory?

He might need it, but he hated every single minute of the estrangement.

The painters dolled up the first floor of his house on Monday. By Tuesday, he was ready to furnish the first-floor rooms. When boxes and crates arrived on schedule, he wanted Melonie there with him. Opening things, laughing over this and that.

But Melonie wasn't there.

Silence claimed the little house.

Birdsong filled the air outside, but inside, where her laughter had once brought life back to a place of sorrow, the quiet grew thick around him.

He put together two cribs with no help.

He laid the pretty oval rug on the girls' floor, then had the two delivery guys position the white dressers where Melonie had indicated on her design.

Double toy shelves.

A play table.

Two cribs.

They'd given the girls the biggest bedroom, but by the time he was done, the room seemed full. Yet empty. Because Melonie wasn't sharing the joy of preparation with him.

Gilda had given Melonie's friend permission to film some of the renovation.

They hadn't asked him.

Just as well.

He'd have offered his opinion and messed things up even more than they already were. By the time he and the guys tackled demolition on Thursday, he was regretting his decision to step away.

He grabbed a sledgehammer and began demo on the Hardaway home interior with three hired hands. For the next week he'd be buried in breaking things down, shoring them up and putting structural beams into place. And moving the girls into the Middleton house.

There wasn't time to think of anything else, including Melonie, but he couldn't seem to think of anything *but* Melonie—and that was a whole other problem.

"You guys are amazing. I can't believe how much you've gotten done." Melonie came through the front door of the Hardaway house on Saturday and gave the four-man crew a thumbs-up. "You guys don't mess around, do you?"

"Jace doesn't let us up for air, but he keeps having pizza and sandwiches delivered," one man offered.

"And muscle cream and ibuprofen," laughed another man.

"So that takes the edge off," added Spike Bennett, an older carpenter who lived in town. "Food, coffee and pain relief."

"He's a considerate guy." She didn't look at Jace when she said it. He was considerate. When he wanted to be. But no matter how much she missed their time together, she wasn't anyone's casual acquaintance. Especially when there wasn't one thing casual about those kisses.

She turned to Jace, pretending she didn't care. "I've got a favor to ask you."

"Sure."

"I've got to get some final quiet work done before we have the building inspector look at these plans, and Pine Ridge Ranch is anything but quiet right now with wedding plans, people and babies. Can I spend Monday at your place?"

"Yes, of course."

"Perfect. Thank you." It wasn't perfect. Perfect would be having his arm around her shoulders. Drawing her in. Laughing at Ava's attitude and Annie's questioning looks. Cuddling on a sofa. Tucking the girls into bed.

Ezra called her name from the door. "I got some great demo and clean-up shots this morning. Can I get a few of you guys interacting amid the rubble?"

"Sure." She complimented the guys again, this time for the camera. And when she asked Jace about working at his house, he answered in a cool, polite tone as if the whole thing was a bother.

That made her all the more determined to put the polish on this project. Not to show him up. But to show her stuff because no one would ever get to consider her a bother again.

Jace motioned toward the darkening sky midday on Monday. "It looks like the forecasters got it right this time," he told Spike. He'd hired the older man to double-team the Hardaway project, and no one knew carpentry and construction better than Spike. "That's a mean-looking sky heading our way."

"It's fierce, for certain. Makes you glad the roofs are done. And we've got this place just about ready to renovate, but I think we need to sit down with Melonie and go over those design plans. I work better with a clear picture. Tonight, maybe?" Spike had mentioned this before and he'd put him off.

"Should work." Chin down, Jace pried nails out of the hardwood flooring. He'd deliberately delayed going over the plans with Melonie, but he'd have to prioritize it now. Spike shouldn't have to ask. He should have set the meeting in stone. What if they needed to make extensive alterations to her ideas?

He'd been able to cut the other two men loose after Saturday's work. Now it was him and Spike to complete the renovation, guided by Melonie's vision and her camera-hugging friend.

Thunder rumbled. They'd been dry for two weeks, not unusual for Idaho summers, but when things got too dry, wildfires became a concern. And things dried out real quick in a mountain summer.

Another flash of lightning commanded his attention as the threatening sky pitched their way.

He put aside the flash of concern. The girls were safe and sound. Gilda was at Pine Ridge making jam with Corrie. Melonie?

Nope. Not his concern, but he had to shove the niggle of worry aside with mental force. She was at his house, and from the looks of the sky, the storm was rolling in north of his place. She'd be fine.

Focusing on demolition details, he ignored the growing tumult. There was work to do and one way or another, he meant to do it.

Chapter Sixteen

Melonie glanced outside as the light dimmed. Dark clouds skirted north of her, rolling across the valley like a well-done movie shot. She hadn't bothered checking the weather report that morning, but when her phone indicated a storm alert, she frowned. It looked like the storm would narrowly miss Jace's house, but Pine Ridge Ranch was in its path. The brewing storm was definitely going to make the folks over there sit up and take notice.

A sharp crackle of lightning split the air, followed by a swift, harsh crash of thunder. No rain, but the busy side of the storm had found her.

Lightning struck close again, almost sizzling, and when the thunder followed quickly, a gust of welcome, cool wind filled the kitchen.

The horses whinnied. One? Both? She wasn't

sure, and the sound was muffled, like it came from the barn.

Lightning cracked again, with a distinctive *snap!*

Thunder followed instantly.

Her pulse quickened. Her heart beat a little harder in her chest.

To the south, the sky was deceptively clear. The town of Council was getting glorious sun.

But to the north, Mother Nature was unleashing her fury. Melonie's visibility was obscured by the intense storm, even though the rain didn't reach Jace's place.

Were the girls all right at Rosie's little house? Was Zeke there, or at the big house with Lizzie?

She started pacing the room, fighting nerves. She'd been in storms before, but the wide-open valley gave her a better vantage point, and this storm was raging over people she loved. Still, it was just a thunderstorm. She was being silly.

She moved back toward the computer.

The wind blew again, shifting the ruffled topper she'd put on the kitchen window. And with the wind came smoke.

Not just the scent of a distant campfire.

Smoke blew into the newly renovated house, a thick cloud of it, smelling foul and rancid.

She slammed the window shut, grabbed her

phone and dashed outside, where her heart managed to jump straight into her throat.

The barn, a scant hundred feet from the house, was on fire. And Jace's two horses were inside, crying in piteous equine voices.

Her heart raced. Her palms went hot and damp.

She hit 911 and spoke quickly as she tried to open the gate. When the gate gave her trouble, she scaled the fence and landed with a thud on the other side. "Barn fire, 1727 Crossing Corners Road. Lightning strike, spreading quickly."

"Are there people in the building?"

She ran across the paddock. "No. Two horses."

"We've got Engine Company Two responding."

She pocketed the phone.

Bubba and Bonnie Lass didn't have time to wait for fire engines and big, brawny men.

They had her, and she knew how badly horses hated fire. And how much she feared horses.

Her gut seized. Her breath went shallow.

She stared at the barn as the raging fire swept from north to south along the back wall. Stacks of dried hay and straw fed the flames. To her right were the horse stalls, but the horses hadn't been closed in that morning. They'd been walking the paddock when she arrived. So they weren't closed in the stalls but they were in the barn, and they weren't wearing halters.

God, give me courage. And don't let me fail.

She whispered the prayer as she grabbed a lead rope from the hooks inside the broad, open doors, and didn't think. She didn't dare think, because if she did, she'd be useless and she couldn't afford to be useless now.

Bubba stood in front of Bonnie Lass as if sheltering her, and when she slipped the noose around his neck, he came right along, outside. She prayed Bonnie Lass would follow the old guy's lead, and when she got Bubba upwind of the fire, she tied him to a fence post, then ran back to the barn.

The north end was fully engulfed now. Bonnie Lass was at the other end, near the closed doors. If those doors would open, bringing Bonnie out might not be all that hard.

She ran that way, but when she tried the doors, they wouldn't budge.

Heart racing, she went back to the west-facing entrance, grabbed another lead line and hurried in.

Bonnie Lass backed up farther. She pushed herself into the far corner and stared at Melonie with frightened eyes.

Then she whinnied, only it was more like a scream.

"Easy. Easy, girl."

Bonnie Lass wanted no part of her easy talk. Smoke was pushing their way, and the crackle of fire grew louder. She felt the temperature rising, and still she reached for the horse's face.

Bonnie Lass rose up on her back legs.

Melonie's heart slammed.

Memories grabbed hold of her, of another horse. Another time, only that time it was Melonie in the corner, with no escape. And the horse was big...so big. And so very angry.

Don't think about that now.

This isn't Sweet Red Wine. This is Jace's horse, and she's nice. But scared. Think, Melonie. Think!

"Whoa. Whoa. Whoa." She slipped her hand up Bonnie Lass's face, toward her ears. "There we go, there we go. Good girl."

Her words seemed to help. The words themselves or the tone?

She didn't know and didn't care. She stroked the horse's face again. Would she let her slip on the rope? Should she take time for a halter?

The rising noise of the wind-fed fire nixed that idea and Melonie didn't have to look back to know that her escape route would be cut off soon. "Here, girlie." She'd heard Jace use that term before. "Come on, girlie, let's get out of this place. We've got fresh air waiting for us, right through that door."

She slipped the rope halter up, over Bonnie Lass's ears. The horse shied back.

Melonie hung tight. "Gotta go, girlie. Gotta go." She thought she whispered the words, but maybe not, because the horse shied again.

Smoke billowed up, then at them.

The flames were licking closer. There wasn't time for sweet talk or coaxing. Bonnie Lass either came now or would be left behind.

Melonie put more pressure on the rope as she turned away. "Come along. Come along."

Bonnie Lass rose up. Up. Up.

Don't think about it. Don't remember. Just keep walking.

Melonie didn't turn. She couldn't. The sight of those hooves raised high in the air might undo her and she couldn't afford to be undone now. "Come along, girlie. We've got this."

She didn't have it. The horse came down with a thud, and when she tried to shy away, Melonie tugged the other way, almost to the door. Close to safety. So close. "We've got this."

"We sure do." Strong hands closed above hers on the rope. "Mel, get out there. I'll draw her out. If I can."

Jace.

There, with her, with a pair of strong hands

to help. But she wasn't about to leave now, with the wide opening so close behind them. "On three." She quick-counted to three and with both of them pulling at the same moment, Bonnie Lass stuttered along those last few steps, then cleared the door.

She let go then.

Fire engines were racing their way. Sirens blared, and as they came around the corner, the sight of them...

And the horse's fear...

And the noise...

Brought back all she'd forgotten about that horrible day twenty years before.

The small fire.

The horse.

Being trapped.

And then...

Her heart chugged to a full stop, remembering the sound of the single shot that brought the horse down. And her father, the anger and the disappointment she saw on his face as the prize filly was lying on one side of the barn's corner...

And his brutalized daughter was lying on the other.

"Come on." Jace grabbed hold of Melonie and led her through the gate. "Come out front, we'll be out of the way."

She let herself be led as a myriad of thoughts vied for attention.

"Is your laptop in the house?"

His voice jerked her back to the present. "Yes." Looking up, she realized the house was in danger unless the fire company could keep the flames from spreading. "On the kitchen table. I closed the window."

He stared at her, then brought a cool, soothing hand to her hot face. Her cheek. "Thank you, darlin'. I appreciate it." He ran through the front door, ignoring the scoldings of the first responders, and came back out with her laptop, purse and an armful of family pictures that they'd just rehung on the living room walls.

"Got the important stuff," he told the fire chief as he came his way. "Just in case." He set the pictures in his truck with her computer, then started to guide her to the trees as a rescue vehicle pulled in.

She turned back and tugged him that way. "We've got to move the horses, in case they get free. They might go back to the barn. They do that, you know. Sometimes."

"I'll see to that right now," he told her.

"You can't do it alone." She slipped from his hand and started to hurry toward the open end of the paddock. "I couldn't get the gate open." She was talking fast, as if trying to explain why

Bubba was still in proximity to the barn. "It jammed and there wasn't time—"

"I'll help him, Melonie." Heath's voice made her turn. "Lizzie's here. You go sit with her where it's cool, okay?" He locked eyes with her and spoke slow and firm. "You did real good, Mel. It's our turn now."

She blinked up at him.

Then Jace.

She nodded.

But tears were slipping down her cheeks, fast and furious, and there was no way Jace could leave her like that.

"I've got the horses," Heath said. "And here's Ty Carrington. We'll move them to the next section. Ty?"

"I'm in." A tall, broad man strode their way, and he and Heath went to draw the horses to a safer area.

"Hey, hey. Don't cry, Melonie." Jace drew her into his chest. Into his heart as her tears soaked the front of his plain white cotton T-shirt.

"I couldn't get away."

He frowned, not understanding, but not willing to break in, either.

"There was a fire, not a big one like this, a small one, and it wasn't even that close. I went to look and when I turned around, she charged me. She was big, Jace." She drew back as if trying to convince him. "So big. And all I could see was her anger and her fear and those hooves. And then I couldn't get away, I was boxed in, and she just kept kicking me. It seemed to last forever and no matter what I did, or how small I got, she wouldn't stop hurting me."

The scar on her face.

His chest went tight. "She hurt you?"

Her breath caught, then softened. And for several seconds, she breathed in and out as if calming herself. The maneuver seemed to work, and that probably meant it was well practiced. "She pummeled my head. Broke several ribs. Bruised my whole body. And mangled my cheek. My jaw was wired shut for weeks and I had multiple surgeries to put things back together."

He prayed mentally.

For her strength, for her well-being, for her peace. No wonder she steered clear of horses and barns. And he'd been willing to believe she was just a spoiled little rich girl who never had to prove herself in anything. Or to anyone.

"I knew I was going to die," she said softly. "I heard voices, screaming and yelling, but they couldn't pull her away. They couldn't get her off and the alley was blocked. And then I heard the gunshot."

Help her, Lord. Please help her.

She kept her face pressed against his shirt,

against his chest and he held her there, wishing he could do something—anything—to make this better. "I'd forgotten so much of this," she went on. "The details of it. They said it was because of the concussion. That I might never remember, and I didn't care because who wants to remember that? But then, today." She drew back as the firefighters surrounded the barn and house, pumping water through thick, heavy hoses. "I could see it in my head. I had to tell myself that Bonnie Lass wasn't Sweet Red Wine, that she was a nice horse. A good horse. She had to be because she was yours and you wouldn't keep a bad animal on the farm."

"Never."

"And then I remembered the shot. And my father's face, so angry. So disappointed. So sorry to have to put that beautiful animal down because a little girl went where she wasn't supposed to go."

Jace gripped her shoulders. "Is that what you think? That he was angry about putting down a rogue horse?"

She looked up at him. Confusion drew her eyebrows down. "He was angry about it. That horse was worth a quarter-million dollars. Anyone would be angry about it."

"Did your father hesitate, Melonie?"

She knew he didn't because she heard his

voice, screaming…and then the shot. She shook her head.

"He wasn't mad or disappointed in you. I'm going to guess he was absolutely furious with the horse."

He was wrong, of course, but Lizzie came to her side at that moment. "Jace is right." She had a cool, wet cloth in her hand. Reaching out, she applied it to Melonie's right cheek. The chill of the cloth soothed the heated skin. "Dad has a laundry list of faults, we all know that, but he wasn't ever mad at you, Melonie. It was the horse. He bought her, thinking they could gentle her. They couldn't, she was a crazy girl, and I don't think he ever got over blaming himself for what happened. He made everyone promise not to talk about it unless you brought it up."

Was Lizzie right? Had Melonie spent two decades carrying around guilt about something that was never her fault?

The fact that it was a distinct possibility shamed her. "And I never brought it up."

Lizzie acknowledged that with a sad smile and a warm hug. "Who would, sweetie? I never dreamed you blamed yourself for what happened. I just figured the trauma was enough to make you go off horses and barns forever, and it wasn't like Dad was about to win any Father of the Year awards. And yet today—" She shifted her gaze to where Heath and Ty Carrington were putting a firm fence between the horses and the fire. "You were a true hero. I honestly can't imagine how you did it, Mel. But you did, and I'm proud of you."

So was Jace. Proud and grateful. She'd faced her greatest fears for him, after he'd been acting like a first-class jerk to her.

The EMT came alongside them right then. "Let's have a look here, missy." The older woman pointed to the rescue wagon. "I want to check your breathing and vitals. Then you can go back to hugging your boyfriend."

"I'll be right there with her," Jace promised.

"But the fire—"

He kept his arm looped around her shoulders as he led her to the waiting ambulance. "It's only a building. As long as you're okay, nothing else matters, Mel."

And he hoped she'd give him the chance to prove that he meant it.

Chapter Seventeen

The sting in Melonie's cheek had eased by Wednesday. A surface burn, like a moderate sunburn, and nothing more.

"Rosie's got a doctor's appointment for Jo Jo today, so we're keeping the girls here." Corrie washed up Annie and then Ava when the girls had finished breakfast. Lizzie had taken advantage of the early morning sun and was giving Zeke a ride on Honey Bunny, one of the ranch stock horses. "Do you have to get to Gilda's?"

"No. Supplies are scheduled to be delivered today and the men will start rebuilding the upstairs tomorrow. Jace is moving sheep right now."

"Well, I wonder if these two would like a nice walk in that big, fancy stroller we've got out there. Maybe see what their cowboy daddy is doing?"

Melonie laughed.

The stroller was big, all right, but not one bit fancy. Rosie had found it at a garage sale the previous year when she first started watching the twins. It was bulky, but the thick tires worked on farm lanes, and that meant everything around here. "I'll take them. I could use a walk myself. We can go see Jace in action and maybe meet some sheep."

They fastened the girls into their seats. Ava might have beaten Annie at walking, but Annie was part monkey when it came to climbing. She'd wiggle her way out of that stroller seat in a heartbeat without the safety buckle firmly fastened.

"I've got to get that cake in the oven," Corrie reminded her. "Are you okay on your own with them?"

"They're way smaller than the horse I tackled a few days ago. I think we're okay."

Corrie laughed, then hugged her. "My brave girl! See you when you get back."

Ezra was editing video in the first-floor equine-barn office. He'd gotten some great preliminary shots and a short but poignant one-on-one interview with Gilda—an interview he wouldn't let anyone see, which meant it was good. Real good.

She pushed the stroller forward.

June had started out with kelly green grass rolling across the hills, like the Irish countryside pictures her grandmother had always loved. As the end of the month closed in, the green had deepened. Dandelions nodded yellow heads all around the farmyard. Clumps of perennials were grouped in random spots, not yet blooming.

It was a beautiful place. Different than Kentucky, more rugged. Less pristine, yes. But it called to her like it was meant to be. Like she belonged there. But how hard would it be to be here, day after day, watching Jace raise these babies from afar? When he'd held her a few days ago, she'd sensed his caring emotion.

But between the fire's aftermath, smoke damage to the bedroom wing of the house and the final bits of teardown at Gilda's, she'd barely seen him. Now he was moving sheep for Heath, making ready for the next round of lambs, which were due soon.

He was at the far side of the nearest pasture when they approached. He sat tall in the saddle on a Pine Ridge Ranch horse, and the straight lines of his back, his easy hands and the tilt of his black cowboy hat made him look like an ad in a Western magazine.

He saw them. He raised a hand in a salute, then headed their way, taking care to not disturb the ewe and lamb groupings.

He pulled up in front of them and looked down, smiling.

He shouldn't be so handsome. So strong. So good and nice.

He climbed down off the horse, let it graze, then crossed the last few feet to them. He was on one side of the sheep fence.

She was on the other.

He fixed that by jumping the fence as if it was nothing. "You gals out for a midday stroll?" He smiled at her, then the girls.

Ava babbled, waving both hands, then she shrieked at the sheep like a little banshee.

Annie looked up at him and simply grinned. Her whole face lit up, without needing to make a scene about it.

Melonie nodded while the girls flirted with him in their distinct ways. "It was too nice to stay inside, but Ava doesn't like the feel of grass under her feet."

"A trait she'll need to lose to be happy on a ranch," Jace teased the baby, and Ava giggled as if sharing the joke.

"And Annie said she wanted to come see her daddy. So I said sure."

"You did?"

She'd been looking down at the girls.

The husky note in his voice made her look up. And when she did, she didn't want to look away from those warm, brown eyes. "Well, sure, it's wonderful for them to see what you do. What it takes to build a place or herd sheep or cut hay."

He leaned closer. "Do I dare hope that you like coming to see me, too? Maybe a little bit?"

Her heart stutter-stepped.

Like coming to see him? Love was more like it. "I believe you've known that all along, Jace. But then you started acting like a jerk, and—"

He kissed her.

He didn't wait, didn't ask, just wrapped those big arms around her and drew her in. And when he was done kissing, her, he kissed her all over again. "I'm sorry I was a jerk. I saw you and Ezra and knew you had dreams and goals that went way beyond an old six-room house in western Idaho. I didn't want to face the thought of you leaving. So I pulled back."

She leaned back against his arm and poked him. "Did it ever occur to you to ask me?"

"You'd already told me how you wanted to do your show, showing off your skills. And that drawl you tried so hard to lose. I find that drawl to be a mighty pretty thing, Melonie Fitzgerald," he added, sending a look her way that set her pulse humming.

"Why, cowboy…" She batted her eyelashes to match the Southern drawl. "You flatter me."

His grin widened. "Woman, you talk like that

and I will be at your beck and call. I'm pretty sure I'm going to be at your beck and call anyway, Melonie. And if that means following you to Kentucky—"

"You would follow me to Kentucky?" She didn't even try to mask her surprise.

He didn't hesitate at all. "Anywhere, Mel. Just as long as you don't mind being a carpenter's wife and a mother to two little girls. I hear Kentucky gets a little hot for a northern guy like me, but I can adjust. Given a little time and encouragement," he added another kiss, and when he finally eased back, she laid her head against his chest.

"What about staying with me right here in Shepherd's Crossing?"

He pulled back and lifted a brow. "I don't get it."

"What if the producers were so in love with the pilot that they're interested in doing the show with a Western twang instead of a Southern drawl? That I get to stay here with you and raise two little Western girls?"

"You're staying?"

"I believe I just said that."

He picked her up and whirled her around, then set her down when Annie burst into tears. "Sorry, darlin', sorry. Daddy's just a little excited, I didn't mean to scare you." He unclasped her safety belt and withdrew the crying baby from the stroller.

Melonie reached down, unclipped Ava's seat belt and did the same with her. Then she reached into her pocket now that Annie had calmed, pulled out her phone and stretched her hand out and up. "All right, you guys. Our first family selfie. Say 'cheese.'"

The word activated the camera function, and when she held out the image for Jace to see, he put an arm around her shoulders and tugged her close. Ava was in her right arm. Annie was perched on his left hip. And they were the absolute image of a happy couple.

"I love it, Melonie. And—" he eased around and rubbed his forehead against hers, gently "—I love you. And despite the fact that you've already kind of asked me, will you marry me, Melonie? Be my wife? And help me raise these precious little girls?"

"I will," she assured him. "Oh, I absolutely will! But we have to wait because I don't want to mess up Lizzie's wedding plans."

"What if the last thing I wanted to do was wait?" he asked then. "And what if we shared their wedding?"

"Say what?"

"What if we have a double wedding with

Heath and Lizzie and we all do that happily-ever-after thing?"

Was he joking?

One look at his face said he wasn't.

"Just so you know, I already ran it by them and they were fine with the idea."

She wasn't sure if she should kiss him or smack him.

She'd spent a lifetime longing to be loved and cherished not for what she was, a rich man's daughter, but for who she was.

And she'd found that right here in the rugged hills and valleys of western Idaho in the arms of the best man she'd ever known.

She reached up and pressed her lips to his mouth. "I love you, Jace. Just in case we get too busy with these two and I forget to tell you."

He grinned down at her. "I know you do, darlin'. But it's sure sweet hearing you say it out loud."

A sheep baaed in the background. Then another one joined in. He eyed the pasture, then her as he tucked Annie back into her side of the stroller. "Duty calls, but I'll look forward to more of that kissin'-and-huggin' stuff tonight. And you little gals be good for your mama, all right?"

More sheep began blatting. A border collie

loped his way, as if wondering what was taking so long.

He hopped back over the fence while she settled Ava into her seat. And when he rode uphill, he paused midway, deliberate and slow. Then he turned the horse slightly and gave the brim of his cowboy hat a tip with one finger.

A cowboy salute.

She laughed, waved and aimed the stroller back toward the house, wondering how life had turned around so completely in the last few weeks and so incredibly glad it did.

A home. A soon-to-be husband. Jobs for both of them, and the promise of rebuilding Hardaway Ranch into a Middleton home.

And two baby girls, needing someone to love them and care for them and raise them. Just like the Middletons had done for Jace.

Her world had changed in a matter of weeks. From doubt had sprung faith.

What if she hadn't taken Uncle Sean's challenge to move here for a year? She'd have missed God's plans for her. For these girls. For Jace, her beloved.

A rooster crowed from the chicken coop west of her. He crowed again, and she laughed.

It wasn't their highfalutin' Kentucky horse farm.

It was better.

And she was here, with a bright new chance at faith, hope and love. And, of course, the greatest of these...

She leaned down and kissed the twins' soft, sweet cheeks...

Was love.

Epilogue

Melonie rolled over, spotted the clock and flew out of bed. She threw on clothes and rushed downstairs. How had she overslept on today of all days? With so much to do?

She dashed into the empty kitchen.

The rich smell of cowboy blend coffee filled the air, but the little house was quiet.

Too quiet.

Then she caught a glimpse of the front yard.

Balloons bobbed and weaved everywhere. Dozens of bright primary-colored helium balloons were tied to every post and open branch and even the chair handles. Color filled the yard, and as she moved through the front door, Jace looked up.

He grinned and her heart just about melted on the spot. "You did all this? Why didn't you get me up, Jace?"

The girls were running their miniature scooters on the driveway. Back and forth, laughing and giggling.

He cupped her cheeks and kissed her. Long and slow and when he stopped, she leaned in for just a little more.

"You worked so hard to get everything ready for today. For their birthday. I wanted you to get some rest so when I heard them chattering, we moved the crazy outside and began filling balloons."

"It looks amazing."

He looped an arm around her shoulders. "So do you, darlin'. And that coffee smells mighty good. I wouldn't mind if a cup found its way out here. I had one earlier but I didn't want to leave the girls alone to go brew another one."

"I'm on it. And I'll bring out the tablecloths."

Bubba nickered from the far pasture. A lean-to shed gave the pair cover for now. They'd have to see about building a replacement barn before winter set in.

But that wasn't a concern today.

Today their soon-to-be adopted daughters turned one year old, and they'd invited friends and family to come have a day of barbecue, babies and children. A celebration of life and love.

"Jace?"

He'd grasped another bunch of balloons and turned, looking absolutely amazing and adorable.

She smiled at him.

He smiled back.

And then she went to make him coffee.

She hadn't had to say a word. He knew. He understood her emotions. Her joy. Because he felt the exact same way.

She brought him out a steaming mug.

He'd tied the balloons to the mailbox post, marking the entrance. A neighbor had loaned them a bounce house for the day, and Gilda had ordered a waterslide. The twins were too small to appreciate it, but everyone else would love it.

He crossed to her, set the coffee aside, then hit a button on his phone.

The music of Glenn Miller filled the air.

He took her into his arms.

The twins giggled and bobbed up and down, their own way of dancing to the music.

And when Jace began leading her across the lawn to the sweet old tune, Melonie followed, step for step. And when the first song wound down, she leaned up, batted her eyelashes against his cheek and made him laugh. Then sigh.

"I am looking forward to spending the rest of my life doing this—" she indicated the yard, the kids and the handsome cowboy with a wave of her hand "—forever. I couldn't ask for anything more, Jace. Except…"

He lifted one eyebrow.

"Another dance? Please."

He smiled. And then began dancing her across the lawn again, as if there weren't a million things to do to get ready for the party.

Because nothing was more important than dancing with his wife.

And she loved that most of all.

* * * * *

Dear Reader,

Life has a way of handing us curves, doesn't it? Sometimes we see them coming and we dodge left, then right. And yet they still come!

Sometimes we're caught unaware, and we're faced with life changes we didn't expect and maybe didn't want.

But faith is our rock. Faith is our solidity, it's the binding force that lets us face those challenges head-on to make a difference.

Melonie knew what she wanted. She'd felt unloved and often unworthy to be loved, even when she knew it wasn't true. Taking a sharp right turn toward Idaho wasn't in her plans, but isn't it funny what God holds in store for us?

Jace was facing a future he didn't want. He'd lost his parents, had no work, and his sister was finding her own life, and he could do nothing to stop the changes.

But when old sorrows intervened, a whole new path sprang open.

Sometimes our deepest regrets spawn unexpected opportunities.

I hope you loved this wonderful story, set in the gorgeous hills and valleys of western Idaho, a place that drew men and women courageous enough to settle a land that can be harsh yet amazingly giving.

I hope to hear from you! Email me at logan-herne@gmail.com, friend me on Facebook, where I love to play and pray and talk farm stuff with you, or stop by my website, ruthloganherne.com, and check out what's going on in books or at the pumpkin farm!

And may the sweet Lord bless and keep you, not just today but in all days!

With love,
Ruthy

Get 4 FREE REWARDS!

We'll send you 2 FREE Books plus 2 FREE Mystery Gifts.

Love Inspired® Suspense books feature Christian characters facing challenges to their faith... and lives.

FREE
Value Over
$20

Get 4 FREE REWARDS!

We'll send you 2 FREE Books
plus 2 FREE Mystery Gifts.

2018 LOVE INSPIRED CHRISTMAS COLLECTION!

You'll get 1 FREE BOOK and 2 FREE GIFTS in your first shipment!

This collection is guaranteed to provide you with many hours of cozy reading pleasure with uplifting romances that celebrate the joy of love at Christmas.

YES! Please send me the first shipment of the 2018 Love Inspired Christmas Collection consisting of a FREE LARGER PRINT BOOK and 3 more books on free home preview. If I decide to keep the books, I'll pay just $20.25 U.S./$22.50 CAN. plus $1.99 shipping and handling. If I don't cancel, I will receive 3 more shipments, each about a month apart, consisting of 4 books, all for the same low subscribers-only discount price plus shipping and handling. Plus, I'll receive a FREE cozy pair of Holiday Socks (approx. retail value of $5.99)! As an added bonus, each shipment contains a FREE whimsical Holiday Candleholder (approx. retail value of $4.99)!

☐ 286 HCN 4330   ☐ 486 HCN 4330

Name (please print)

Address   Apt. #

City   State/Province   Zip/Postal Code

Mail to the **Reader Service:**
IN U.S.A.: P.O. Box 1867, Buffalo, NY. 14240-1867
IN CANADA: P.O. Box 609, Fort Erie, Ontario L2A 5X3

READERSERVICE.COM

Manage your account online!
- Review your order history
- Manage your payments
- Update your address

> **We've designed the**
> **Reader Service website**
> **just for you.**

Enjoy all the features!
- Discover new series available to you, and read excerpts from any series.
- Respond to mailings and special monthly offers.
- Browse the Bonus Bucks catalog and online-only exculsives.
- Share your feedback.

Visit us at:

ReaderService.com